A
Lesson for
the *Teacher*

JULIE C. ROUND

OLDSTICK BOOKS

First published in 2016 by
Oldstick Books
18 Wiston Close
Worthing BN14 7PU

A CIP Catalogue of this book is available from
the British Library

ISBN: 978-0-9557242-8-2

Front cover images:
© Adobestock | one (*Vespa Girl*)
© iStockphoto | chuwy (*Background*)

Cover design and typeset in Sabon 11pt by
www.chandlerbookdesign.co.uk

Printed in Great Britain by
4 Edge Limited

Also by
Julie C. Round

Lane's End

Un-Stable Lane

The Third Lane

Never Run Away

Never Pretend

*For Jan, Marion,
Ann and Chris*

1

LESSONS

Margaret

I was eighteen years old and never been kissed.

Well, that wasn't exactly true. A boy from school had taken me home after a tiddlywinks match and tried to kiss me on the front porch – but the scent of his aftershave was so overpowering it made me feel sick and I pushed him away.

And now, here I was, clinging to the leather jacket of a boy I had met only once, travelling by motor bike to a venue in Southend to hear a concert by Billy Fury.

What had made me so reckless?

I didn't really see myself as girl friend material. My heart was set on going to college and becoming a schoolteacher. I wanted a career.

I wasn't the kind of girl boys looked at twice. I was short and dumpy with brown hair and a wide mouth. My family called me 'mouse,' and I suppose I had always been quiet, yet I longed to be a leader rather than a follower and saw teaching young children as a way to achieve that.

For my first taste of independence I had selected a teacher training college. This was sited in an ivy covered mansion in extensive grounds in Essex. It was far enough from my home in Middlesex to feel different but near enough to get there in one day by Green Line bus.

"You are on the first floor with Tamsin Greene and Georgina Mason – Room 26," said the woman at the desk when I had wheeled my case into the college foyer.

Tamsin and Georgina had already chosen their beds and started unpacking. Once I had introduced myself as Margaret Jones we compared our course choices.

Georgina (Georgie – she requested) was specialising in Sport, Tamsin, in Art, but we would be together for the lectures in Education and Child Development.

I studied my two room mates. They couldn't have been more different- Tamsin, thin, with dark auburn hair in a 'Cleopatra' bob, bright clothes and high boots – Georgie, tall, statuesque, with long, blonde hair.

I unrolled my poster of Elvis Presley and fixed it to the door of my locker.

Then I hid my pyjamas under my pillow. I had made them myself from blue cotton with white polka dots but had a feeling they might be mocked, especially if the other girls had nightdresses.

"The bathroom's next door," said Georgie. "You'd think they would be en suite."

"It's a bit daunting, isn't it?" I responded.

"We'll be fine," said Tamsin, "Especially if there's somewhere in the village that's fun."

* * *

There was, the village hall held weekly dances. Tamsin and I were eager to try out new dance steps but Georgie didn't jive. She just waited for the slow tunes.

On Saturday two boys came up to Tamsin and me and asked if they could have a dance.

The taller of the two took Tamsin and I was left with a stocky, red faced lad who reminded me of Tommy Steele. Still, beggars couldn't be choosers, could they?

When the music stopped Tamsin had disappeared.

"Are you two up at the college?" asked my partner.

"Yes, I'm Meg – and you are?"

"Bob. I work at the garage."

"You sell cars?"

"I wish. No, I fix them – but I prefer bikes, motor bikes. Would you like a ride sometime?"

"I would, if it's safe."

"Of course it is. I'll bring a helmet for you. How about tomorrow?"

"Well, I should be writing an essay but I could meet you back here at two, after lunch. Boys aren't allowed in the college." I replied, surprised that someone had found me interesting enough to see again.

"Fine, that's a date." he said and disappeared with a wave.

I had decided to wear trousers for my trip with Bob. The motor bike looked very heavy and the noise it made was surprisingly loud. I clung on round his waist and found the experience quite exhilarating.

Riding like that made me feel so close to him that when we reached the shore it seemed quite natural for us to continue the embrace.

His kiss landed on my cheek. He'd aimed for my mouth and missed, which made me laugh, but seeing his expression of dismay I relented, moved into his arms and kissed him properly.

He held me close and nuzzled into my neck and I clung to him, trying not to breathe in the mixture of oil and perspiration.

Then, pulling away slowly, I asked, "Can we find somewhere sheltered?" hoping he'd realise I meant a café. I'd enjoyed being cuddled but needed to find out much more about him before we went any further.

We had a quick cup of tea and a burger before the concert started but Bob looked rather uncomfortable and had to rush out half way through.

He returned some time later looking sheepish and said very little until we left the pavilion when he confessed he had been 'caught short' and was suffering with a stomach ache. We rode home rather faster than I liked but he deposited me at the gates of the college and drove off without further explanation. He did not ask to see me again.

My date had been a disaster.

For the rest of the term I resolved to concentrate on my studies. Tamsin still went to the dances but Georgie and I stayed behind and buried our noses in books. We were very aware that we would soon be visiting schools and studying child development. Before that we were to be educated as to how people in other occupations spent their time. It seems someone, somewhere, felt we needed lessons in life outside school.

Tamsin

Our shared room in college had been a hoot and the year had been quite unexpected as it was mostly 'Community Studies' a device to fill the gap between school child and school ma'am with an introduction to 'real life.'

This took the form of of day trips to farms, factories and offices – to find out how other people earned their living. Then each of us chose a subject for further study.

I chose travel agency, Meg chose nursing and Georgie chose hairdressing. These in depth studies almost made me change my mind about my future career.

In the second year we were split up and housed in lodgings in the town. I had encouraged Meg to spend the summer on a farm with me where we picked beans, sorted sprouts and lived like 'land girls ' sleeping on bunks in a barn, but we saw less of each other at college.

When we had our first teaching practice I had a class of infants and they were as good as gold, sponging round leaves we had gathered and making pictures for display.

Meg struggled to instill discipline on a class of nine year olds and felt like giving up, but Georgie said it was just part of the learning process.

That summer Meg and I helped at a summer school. We thought we would be organising activities but we seemed to spend more time cooking and washing up.

Our final year saw us installed in newly built blocks of single rooms, each with their own bathroom. It felt like luxury and the fresh surroundings helped us to concentrate on passing our final exams.

Each of us succeeded and we began to apply for teaching positions. We had a probationary year to do and then we would be fully qualified teachers.

Margaret

Studying other occupations, especially life as a nurse, convinced me that I had chosen the right career.

I was happy having the day divided into time slots by bells. I liked the sense of order and I loved teaching children to read. I just had to get over my initial nerves.

While my first teaching practice had been difficult, it was probably because the school was modern, trendy, with children in groups, and had been used regularly for students and so we did not have the respect they gave to their usual teachers.

The last school I worked in was more old fashioned, with desks facing the front, and I managed to keep the children's attention while the inspector was watching me.

It was a relief to find all three of us passed, with Georgie gaining a distinction in sport.

It was the end of our final year. We had celebrated with a meal in a local pub when I had my first taste of real champagne and was not impressed.

I was sorry to leave the college and it felt very strange stepping back into the role of obedient daughter.

I had changed, but my parents hadn't. They still worked hard in our shoe shop all week and spent each Sunday at the cricket. My father was the captain of the local team and mother organised the teas. I went with them out of habit, not concerned about the game but happy to be out in the fresh air with people who were enjoying themselves.

I helped set out the teas and then sat in a deck chair to wait for the last over. The home side were fielding and they had a new bowler that I hadn't seen before.

He was tall, broad shouldered and dark, with wavy hair that he had to brush out of his eyes.

I wondered what he would look like close to. He moved well as he ran up to bowl, his eyes fixed on the batsman, his body ready to pounce if the ball was returned to him. The batsman swung at the ball and there was a resounding 'whack.'

I watched the ball soar into the air and then drop – right into the hands of a distant fielder. There was a cheer from the observers in the seats around me and they began to stir.

I jumped up and hurried inside.

"Someone's out. Caught on the boundary," I called out.

"They'll be in for tea now," and they were.

Nigel

I rolled my shoulder and pushed my hair out of my eyes. I need a haircut, I thought, although most women liked a man to have a bit of a mane.

I couldn't help looking at myself in the pavilion window as I strode up the steps and through the open doors.

That had been a satisfactory start. I'd made my mark

in the first match for the side. This was a new team for me and I was sure I could be an asset.

"Well done, Nigel." The captain patted me on the back and led me to the table. "Tuck in, son. You've earned it."

"I'll just wash up, captain," I replied. "See you in a mo."

It was when I returned, my hands cleaned and my hair combed, that I noticed the girl.

She moved easily between the tables, her long brown curls tied back in a white alice band. She looked young and vulnerable, but curvy, with a ready smile. How would I describe her? Wholesome, I thought, definitely good enough to eat.

I brought another chair to the table and flashed a smile at her when she offered me tea. "That would be perfect" I said.

Margaret

I blushed. He looked too much like Elvis Presley – but slimmer, more chiselled, with mocking brown eyes. He made me feel uncomfortable, exposed, but, at the same time curious about him. I had to say something. I went back into the kitchen for a plate of cakes and asked if anyone knew his name. One of the helpers said they thought he was called Nigel. It was enough to give me the courage to approach him.

"That was a neat wicket," I blurted out.

He had his mouth full of sandwich but he winked in recognition of my comment. Then, before I had time to continue the conversation someone from across the table began to talk to him and I was left looking at the back of his head. It wasn't until we had nearly finished clearing up that I suddenly felt a hand on my arm.

"I'm not batting until later," he said. "Come and sit with me? You could fill me in with all the gossip."

"I don't know," I stammered, surprised at gaining his attention.

"Go on. I'm new here. I need to know about the area."

"All right. If you put it like that." I hurried into the kitchen with a pile of plates.

"Nigel has asked me to talk to him until it's his turn to bat," I said to my mother. "Is it OK?"

"Of course, dear. You go on. There's plenty of us here," she replied.

I went outside and took the empty seat next to Nigel, feeling embarrassed, as if everyone was watching me – but as the match got under way it became obvious that actions on the pitch were far more interesting to the people around us.

Nigel's smile seemed reassuring, almost conspiratorial.

"Do you come every week?" he asked.

"In the summer. My father's the captain."

"He's at the crease now. We'd better watch."

"He's not the most exciting opener," I found myself saying. Was I making excuses for him before he'd even got going?

"But he's steady, I bet."

I had to change the subject. "What number do you bat?"

"Number seven. There's time for you to tell me what else serves as amusement round here."

"Most people go into town for excitement. London has so many theatres."

"Yes. I've got tickets for a concert. Would you like to join me? I'd feel better going with someone I knew."

"You don't know me."

"But I might, by then. How about coming for a walk round the field? We can watch the action as we go."

He took my hand to help me out of the chair and then kept hold of it as we walked across the grass. It gave me a feeling of belonging, as if it was only natural to be strolling hand in hand, in spite of the fact that we were almost strangers.

"I know you're Nigel," I said. "I'm Margaret, but my friends call me Meg."

"Well, Meg. Tell me about yourself. Are you working?"

I told him, then, about college and my training; how I planned to be Junior School teacher and how I longed to get away from the shop and be independent.

Nigel was a good listener, but, by the time we had done one circuit of the field, four wickets had fallen and he had to get padded up.

"How many did you get, Dad?" I asked as I sat down next to my father.

"Twenty four," he said. "We should make more than a hundred. I wonder how your new friend bats?"

Was that what he was? I wondered, a friend – or could he be something more?

Nigel made forty six runs before he was bowled out and the home side won the match by fifteen runs. The younger players changed quickly and set off for the pub to celebrate but I usually went home with my parents.

Nigel tapped my shoulder.

"Here's my number," he said. "The concert's next Friday. Can I pick you up?"

"You know where I live?"

"Of course. Over the shop. I'll see you at six o'clock."

My heart was thumping in my chest. This was no boy who was asking me out. This was a real man. He looked so suave in his open necked shirt and light trousers. No man had ever made me feel like this – as if being near him wasn't enough. What would it be like for him to hold me close, I wondered, but he smiled his fascinating smile and left with the others.

I floated on air until I got home to the back store room that had been transformed into a bed sit for my own use.

My parents had tried to give me a private space of my own. My visitors could use the rear door and bypass the shop altogether.

I had to go upstairs for a meal or a bath but I had a toilet and a gas ring. I was almost self sufficient – but I hoped it would only be temporary.

Once on my own, the reality of what I had agreed to hit me. Nigel had invited me to a concert in London. It had to be a classical concert. I didn't listen to classical music. I would be shown up as an ignorant provincial. Worse still – what could I wear? What do people wear to concerts? Did he mention the Albert Hall? Should I wear a long dress? I would have to ask mother. If she didn't know she would know someone who did. How much could I afford to spend?

The whole event was becoming more of a trial than a pleasure.

By Friday evening all the problems were solved. Mother had a long velvet skirt that she shortened to fit me and when we teamed it with a white blouse with frilled sleeves, a cameo brooch and new black patent shoes I felt as elegant as I could hope.

I asked my hairdresser to put my hair up and found a pair of clip on earrings shaped like tiny roses.

"You look beautiful," said father, as I fiddled nervously with my bag.

"Do you think the stole I had for Christmas will be enough?" I asked. "It might not stay warm."

"He'll have a car, won't he, George?" asked mother.

"I guess so. I never noticed. He doesn't look short of a bob or two. Come and wait in the shop. He'll have to park at the front."

Nigel did have a car – a Jaguar.

I gasped in awe at the sleek, shiny body. I had wanted to seem sophisticated but I could only stand, open mouthed, as he eased out of the driver's seat and strolled into the shop.

"Good evening, Mr and Mrs Jones," he said and, turning towards me, continued, "I can see you're ready. You look gorgeous."

"Is this OK?" I asked, timidly.

"Beautiful," he replied. "I've booked a table for a light dinner."

He hadn't told me not to eat but I'd been too nervous to have more than a cup of tea.

Nigel

"What would you like?" I asked as we sat in the restaurant. I was surprised at how attractive she looked with her hair pinned up – even though I wanted to pull out the pins and let it down so that I could run my

12

fingers through it. I imagined the feel of it, soft and silky, the curls moving under my touch, especially if they were tumbling over a pillow.

She was wearing a delicate, floral perfume, not musky, reminiscent of bluebell woods and summer meadows. It wasn't exotic – it brought back memories of childhood holidays – tantalising in a completely different way from the sensuous scents my other lady friends usually wore.

She was looking at the menu. It was in French. Would she need help with her decision?

"What do you suggest?" she asked.

"I'm having salmon mousse, the chicken and the crepes suzettes."

"That sounds lovely. I'll have the same, please."

"Relax," I said soothingly and reached across the table to hold her hand.

She blushed and struggled to seem unconcerned. Great, I was definitely having the desired effect.

"You'll be happy with wine?" I asked.

"I'm afraid red wine gives me a headache."

"Then we'll have white." I beckoned to the waiter.

While we ate I told her a little about my life. I had been to a private school and read economics at university but my passion was sports.

"Have you ever been surfing in Cornwall?" I asked.

"No. We always took our holidays on the south coast."

I couldn't help boasting a little, hoping she would be impressed. "While I was there I did modelling for a while. Just for fashion mags. It didn't last."

"But you still work out?"

"Yes, I've found a boxing club that let me use their gym. I go most days,"

It was satisfying to see the admiration in her eyes.

"I'll leave the car where it is and we'll walk, if that's OK?" I said as we left the restaurant.

"It's not far?"

"No, and you don't have stupidly high heels," I laughed as I took her arm.

"Well, don't stride out. I've only got little legs."

Good, she's relaxed enough to joke with me, I thought, and squeezed her arm, commenting "Lovely little legs."

I was rewarded with a beaming smile.

Margaret

It was a classical concert and after a while all the tunes seemed the same to me. I recognised one or two pieces – 'The Hall of the Mountain King' was especially stirring, but watching a bunch of people sitting playing instruments had never been my choice of entertainment.

I closed my eyes and tried to imagine dancing – any sort of dancing, dancing people, dancing shapes, dancing colours, just to give my mind something extra to concentrate on.

There was a pause in the music and everyone clapped enthusiastically.

"Are you OK, Meg?" Nigel whispered in my ear.

"Yes. I was just lost in the music" I lied.

"It's interval time. Let's stretch our legs. I've ordered coffee."

"Fine." I tried to clear my mind with a shake of the head and followed him to the bar.

"Darling!" screeched a stick thin woman with a fur

stole over a glittering golden dress. "Nigel, my pet." She bent forward for a kiss. "How wonderful to see you – and who's your little friend?"

"I'm Margaret" I said, stepping forward before Nigel had time to reply, "And you are?"

"Sophie Dale," interrupted Nigel. "Sophie – Meg, Meg – Sophie."

Sophie raised one eyebrow and waved a tall glass. "We're on champagne tonight, darlings. Why don't you join us?"

"No thanks," replied Nigel and turned towards me. "I'll get our coffees. I won't be a tick."

He took Sophie's arm and steered her away. I watched her flick back her head and laugh at something he said. Suddenly my confidence evaporated and I felt mousy and awkward. These weren't my kind of people and this wasn't my kind of place. I would tell Nigel I had a headache and wanted to go home.

"Sorry about that," he said when he returned with the coffees. "She's usually at the theatre, not so much here. It depends on who she's with."

"Nigel, I'm getting a headache. I don't want to spoil your night but I'd rather leave now."

"That's OK. If it isn't a treat it isn't worth staying. I'll take you back. I've heard it all before."

"I'm sorry to have been a wet blanket."

"Don't fret. Next time you can come to my place for dinner and you can listen to whatever you like."

"I can?"

"Yes. I'm not a bad cook and as long as it's not jazz, I'll play anything."

"My taste is a little more modern."

"All the better. You can educate me."

He smiled down at me and I felt warm with gratitude. He wanted to see me again! He'd been a perfect gentleman and even when I'd ruined his night, he still liked me.

In fact, he showed how much he liked me by stopping the car just before we reached the shop and, leaning towards me, placed his hand on my shoulder.

"A goodnight kiss?" he enquired as his face neared mine.

I couldn't have refused him even if I had wanted to and I didn't want to. My body had been tensing up in anticipation of such a move the nearer we got to home.

I folded my arms round his neck and our lips met. I wanted to drink him in, capture his essence, to keep him alive in me until the next time.

I had never felt such a rush of passion but Nigel looked flushed, as if he hadn't expected quite such a reaction. He gave a quick look round to check if we were being watched and then seemed to regain his composure.

Gently he moved my arms from his neck and gave me a soft kiss on the cheek.

"Save it, darling," he whispered. "Save it for next time."

"When?" I asked.

"Saturday. I'll pick you up at six. We'll have the whole evening together."

He drove up to the shop.

"Thank you, Nigel. Thank you for everything."

He got out and walked round the car to open my door. "Goodnight, Meg," he said.

16

The blast of cool air made me shiver. I stood, hesitating, by the shop doorway. I didn't want the night to end.

He didn't wait. He drove away swiftly and I was left with only the light from the street lamp to show the way round to the rear entrance.

Next time I'll bring a torch, I thought, as I went through the back yard and let myself into my room.

Tamsin

The interview was a breeze.

Once Georgie had told me she'd got a job in a Grammar School in Maidstone, taking Sport and Geography, and suggested I join her in renting a house, my problems were solved.

After all, with my father in Scotland with his fancy woman and my mother shacked up with a new man, who already had two children, there was no way I could go home to Portsmouth, was there?

Moving to Kent seemed like the ideal solution.

Of course I had to tone down my new orange hair and wear reasonably sensible clothes, but I wanted to be true to myself so I wore coloured tights and a fringed leather jacket with a fairly short skirt.

The school in Gillingham was near the dockyard – a dismal building with no field. It looked like it could do with cheering up, but the headmistress was welcoming and offered me the post straight away. I was to teach a class of twenty three infants.

I rang Georgie, who sounded really pleased and arranged to meet me at the weekend to view houses.

As she had a car it seemed sensible to look in Gillingham and we had no trouble finding a place to rent at a reasonable price.

It was a grim looking terraced house but the landlord said we could 'tart it up' inside as much as we liked.

"We'll have to get a new cooker," said Georgie. "I'm not cooking on that filthy thing – and the bathroom needs a thorough clean."

There was no garden, just a tiny yard and the floodlights of the football ground could be seen from the upstairs windows, but we each had a sizeable bedroom.

Georgie took the one with the built-in wardrobe but I didn't mind. I preferred to be at the back.

By the end of August we had moved in, two newly qualified teachers, Miss Georgina Mason and Miss Tamsin Greene, ready to start the next chapter of their lives, and we weren't too far from Meg. We could easily get into London to meet up.

We'd kept her informed of our progress and hoped she'd visit us at half term.

Margaret

The weekend was spent a daze.

I should have been preparing for the start of term in September but, instead, I revisited every second of Friday night and then began to plan for the following Saturday.

I wanted to impress Nigel. I needed to buy something new to wear, something feminine and fashionable.

But Monday came and my father asked if I would help in the shop while mother visited the dentist.

It was the end of the school holidays and I knew we would be inundated with harassed mothers trying to get their children into sensible lace-up shoes instead of the fancy ones they wanted.

Still, we had the xray machine to measure foot sizes and the boys, especially, enjoyed that experience.

It was ten thirty when a tall, lanky young man with untidy sandy hair entered the shop.

He had a folder in his hands and a serious expression on his face that hardly changed when I asked if I could help.

"Is the manager around?" he replied.

"Sure, I'll fetch him." I felt rebuffed. Usually a smile from me elicited a more friendly reaction.

My father came through from the back corridor, carrying a couple of boxes.

"Mr. Jones?" said the stranger.

"Yes – and you are?"

"From the Council. My name's Graham Harris. I've come to check the place over. We did send a letter."

"Yes. I remember. Please look round. Margaret will help you if you have any questions."

"I think I'll manage, thanks," came the reply.

What a rude man, I thought as I bent down to pick up the unwanted shoes left by the last customer.

"I see you've got a fluoroscope," remarked the stranger as I walked past him to put the boxes away.

"Yes – if the customer requests it," I replied. "Why? Is there a problem?"

"You know they have been banned in the USA?"

"No, I didn't. Why is that?"

"Too many xrays can be dangerous. I would advise

you to get rid of it. Now I'd like to see the stock room, please."

Well, at least he asked politely, I thought, but this could be tricky.

I led him out into the corridor and along to the bottom of the stairs where the wall was stacked with shelves of boxes. There were so many there were even a few boots on the steps. The whole family were used to walking carefully up the stairs avoiding them but I had a feeling this was not acceptable to my companion.

"That door," he said, pointing to the door to my room. "Isn't that the stock room?"

"It used to be." I felt myself blushing, "But now it's my bed-sitting room."

"And what about fire precautions?"

"There's an extinguisher under the stairs and, as you see, no heater in the hallway."

"Mmm," he said. "Your parents live upstairs?"

"Yes. Did you want to see that?"

"Not now. I think I have seen quite enough. I must talk to Mr Jones before I leave. Thank you."

He had a frown on his face as he turned away from me.

I didn't offer him refreshment. He seemed eager to get away.

I placed the boxes of shoes on the rack and turned to go back into the shop but as I passed the door to the cellar it opened abruptly and struck me in the face.

"Ouch!" I shouted – my eyes filling with tears.

"I'm sorry," the young man said, shutting the door behind him and grasping my arm. "I was just checking the extinguisher. I thought you'd gone into the shop. Please don't cry."

"My nose, you've broken my nose." The pain was making me wince.

"Please don't say that. It's only bruised. It's not bleeding." He held out a tissue.

"Oh, go away!" I snapped. "You're more dangerous than the xray machine and the boxes put together!"

He smiled, then – and I couldn't help thinking how funny I must have looked. Taking the tissue, I rubbed my eyes and blew my nose. It throbbed a little but I didn't really think he'd done much harm.

"I think I'd better be off," he said, "Forgive me, Miss Jones."

"Meg," I corrected. "I'm only Miss Jones to my pupils."

He gave a nod and a weak smile and went through the door to the shop.

I held it open and watched him speak to my father and then waited until he had left before I re-entered the shop.

All the customers had gone and my father was staring at the xray machine.

"I never realised it was dangerous," he said.

"Surely, only if it was used for too long?"

"Well, we did let the children have more than one go on it sometimes. I'm afraid they'll have to do without it. They'll have to be satisfied with our manual measurement systems."

"It's a shame. Maybe we can think of another way of amusing them. Boys really don't like trying on shoes. What else did he say?"

"It's not good news. He thinks stacking the shoes in the corridor is a bad idea. What else can we do? We can't put them in the cellar."

"It's obvious, Dad. I'll have to move out and let you have the store room back. I'll look for a room near the school. If nosey parker Harris lets us alone until Christmas I'm sure I can find somewhere."

"Oh, Meg. Your mother will be so disappointed."

"I had to move out one day. This just means it's a bit sooner than we expected."

Graham

I sat in the van, trying to write a report on the shoe shop that would not mean it had to be closed down.

There were so many safety infringements I hardly knew where to start. Mr Jones had promised to get rid of the fluoroscope but I couldn't believe how they'd managed with all the shoes stacked up in the hallway. Maybe I could look into some kind of mobile shelving that they could put in the shop. It might mean rearranging things, but while the daughter insisted on having her own room there was little option.

They could, perhaps, use an upstairs room but it would be most inconvenient. She must have had a bedroom when she was little. Why couldn't she stay in that?

She was a teacher, she'd said. She was probably a bossy madam. Maybe she wanted privacy to entertain boyfriends. She was attractive enough, in an English Rose sort of way – nothing special, but good humoured, until I'd banged her nose.

What an idiot I was, sometimes – a clumsy, boring clot. What did my sister call me? 'Gawky Graham.' I felt just like that today, and miserable that I might be putting someone's livelihood in danger.

Back in the office I tried to write a report on the shoe shop that would not mean it had to be closed down. Maybe I'd leave it for a week or so. I had plenty of others to write up.

Margaret

When mother came home my father was clearing the boots off the stairs and taking them into the shop.

He'd moved some of the displays to make room for more boxes and taken the fluoroscope out to the back shed.

"At least that gives us a bit more space," he said miserably.

"What happened?" asked mother.

"An inspector came," I answered. "He said the xray machine was dangerous and the boxes shouldn't be stacked in the hall. Don't worry about it. I'll move out as soon as I can find somewhere near my new school."

"Oh, darling – surely that isn't necessary. Tom, there must be a better answer?"

"He seemed pretty sure about everything," said my father.

"He was a stuck-up, irritating squirt," I said, bitterly. "I bet he went back to the office and reported us straight away."

"Well... if it's his job," said my mother.

"Oh Mum. He could have been a bit more understanding. He just told Dad to change things and left."

"He didn't exactly say what would happen when he reported us," said Tom. "He implied that he'd be back to see what progress we had made."

"He needn't bother," I snapped, surprising myself at the vehemence of my retort. What was it about the stranger that irritated me so much?

Was it the way he almost ignored me– or the twinkle in his blue eyes when I finally got his attention?

Don't be stupid, I told myself. There's only one man for me, and that's Nigel, and I need to start thinking what to wear for my dinner date next weekend.

Graham

I was inspecting the kitchen of a café. I may have been employed to check weights and measures but I couldn't help noticing if anything else was wrong.

I didn't like this part of my job. I always found some problem, whether it was poor hygiene, mice or something worse.

But today the place was spotless. The fridges were at the right temperature and there was no sign of infestation.

I praised the owner, found my glasses, and sat in the van to complete my report.

Then my thoughts turned to the other report – the one I hadn't given in.

Was there a way I could help the family sort out their storage problems – or would the feisty young woman I'd met find a solution if only I waited?

I wanted to go back and see how they were getting on, but it felt too soon. I'd wait a couple of weeks into September and then return.

Margaret

I had visited my school and been shown my classroom.

I had a large folder with the syllabus and lesson suggestions. I'd planned out my first week, starting on a Tuesday. I would be attending a staff training day on the Monday.

I was nervous about it – but even more nervous about Saturday night.

Still, it was my opportunity to show how trendy I could be.

I had a pink polo necked top that I liked – and if I teamed that with a short black skirt I'd feel about as fashionable as I could get.

I searched through my record collection for tunes Nigel might like, Adam Faith, Bert Weedon, Cliff Richard, Dusty Springfield – everything seemed so upbeat. I needed something slower, more romantic, like 'Moon River.' I hummed to myself as back-combed my hair. Maybe I should bleach it, I thought, or at least, get highlights. That's what Tamsin would suggest.

Life had such possibilities now. If only I could find a place of my own to live.

Knowing that Georgie and Tamsin had already found a house of their own made me feel left behind, immature. I had two more days of my holiday. Tomorrow I'd go into the next town and start making enquiries.

I had never been in a large block of flats before.

It felt strange walking up flights of stairs and along a long, dark corridor with numbered doors.

Maybe I should have looked at flats with balconies –

not this anonymous block that felt more like a massive hotel than a home.

But I was someone on my own. I couldn't afford a flat. I hadn't even started earning yet. A room would do – and the agent unlocked a door and gestured for me to go inside.

It was smaller than my room at the shop! There was a bed, a wardrobe, a chest of drawers, a chair and a gas ring. There was a tiny sink but no toilet.

I went to the window. I was three floors up and had a view of the park – but how could I live like this? I'd had better facilities at college.

"I'll show you the bathroom, shall I?" asked the agent.

"No thank you. It's very nice, but not quite what I'm looking for," I replied. I could hardly wait to get out. In comparison with the room at the shop it was a cell, a prison - and it made me feel like a bee in a hive.

I'd have to find somewhere better than that or I'd be obliged to remain at home.

I'd put a notice in the newsagent's window. Perhaps a flat share would be a better idea. It wouldn't give me privacy but it would give me more space.

Unless, of course, Nigel asked me to move in with him? The idea thrilled and frightened me.

He didn't live near the school – but, if he was my Mr. Right, I'd find a way to make it work.

I day-dreamed about our future together as I went home on the bus and nearly missed my stop.

Saturday was busy in the shop. Children were buying new shoes for school and my back ached by four o'clock. I went upstairs for a bath.

I felt more like going to sleep than going out and there was a nervous feeling in my stomach that stopped me relaxing.

Then six o'clock arrived and Nigel drew up outside the shop in his Jaguar.

"Take a coat!" my mother called out as I ran down the stairs.

"I will," I replied as I picked up my duffle bag containing the records and some toiletries.

I'd hesitated over nightwear. What would I do if he asked me to stay the night?

I didn't feel ready. I'd have to say no- but the thought of it made me shiver with desire.

His smile as he opened the car door warmed me, and I gave him a peck on the cheek and snuggled back into the comfort of the seat.

"You've got the music?" he enquired.

"Yes. A mixed bag. I hope there's something you like."

"The Beatles?"

"Actually, no. You'll have to wait and see."

He smiled broadly and pulled into the traffic. "Then we've both got mysteries to discover."

I expected Nigel's flat to be stark and masculine looking but, although it was neat and formal, the brown and cream décor was warmed by the aroma of cooking coming from the kitchen.

"Would you like a sherry?" Nigel was asking. "I'll take your coat."

"Thank you. That would be lovely," I replied. "What's for dinner? It smells delicious."

"Veal escalopes. I thought we might be able to get

away with white wine for you and red for me," he laughed.

I took the proffered glass – hoping it would make me feel more at ease. In spite of his humour I still felt at a disadvantage.

He was worldly wise and I had experienced so little – going from school to college – both enclosed environments. I'd not travelled abroad and not encountered many people socially outside the areas of trade and education.

I looked round for a surface on which to put my glass.

The table at the far end of the room was set for two, with three unlit candles in the centre. The cloth was white and the place mats had an intricate abstract design that made me think of the Orient.

Nigel came out of the kitchen behind me. "You like it?" he said ambiguously.

"You've gone to a lot of trouble," I replied, turning to face him as his arms wrapped round my body.

He brushed my neck with his lips. "Mmmm beautiful," he murmured, "but the meal's ready – if you would like to be seated."

"Where can I wash my hands?" I asked, embarrassed again.

"Through the door to the lobby. On the left past the coat rack," he said. "I'll just get the wine."

True to his word, he brought a chilled bottle of white wine and an open bottle of red.

Two glasses were filled by the time I returned and he carried in a dish of fresh vegetables. The potatoes were new, buttered and minted, and as he started to serve me, his body tantalisingly close, the food almost seemed irrelevant. I had come to be with him – not to consume a meal.

"Is the wine sweet enough?" he asked.

"Yes, thank you," I responded, taking another sip.

"Not as sweet as you," he said as he lit the candles and sat opposite me.

That was a bit smarmy, I thought, but the meal looked appetising and he did seem genuinely interested in me.

I told him about the inspector who had come to the shop and my plans to find a room of my own. Neither of us had large portions and I was grateful when the dessert turned out to be cheese, biscuits and grapes, so I could have as little as I liked, although the food had made me thirsty and the wine bottles were soon empty.

Nigel

I cleared the table and started the coffee machine.

"Please make yourself comfortable." I called out.

Margaret had left a pile of records by the music centre. She was admiring my big, soft easy chairs and the long leather settee. I watched as she chose the latter. Then I took in the coffee and left her a cup on a side table and moved to the record player.

I had to smile to myself as I sorted through the records she had brought. I hadn't realised how youthful her tastes were. It almost made me feel old. However, it did give me hope that, for once, I had found myself a virgin. The thought of being her first lover made me impatient for the next stage in their evening.

Eventually I found something that didn't sound as if

we should be up jiving and sat down next to Margaret, putting my arm round behind her and letting my fingers tickle her neck.

I felt a shiver shoot through her and she gasped as if it was unexpected.

"You like that?" I purred.

She nodded. I had rendered her speechless.

Gratified, I bent forward and kissed her – a deep, warm, intense kiss and she seemed to melt into me.

"You're beautiful," I murmured – letting my hand roam over her body. "Such a lovely figure. Show me, please."

I knew she wanted to. I could feel she wanted to be naked, to feel flesh on flesh.

She pulled her top over her head and gasped as I stretched behind her and undid her bra.

She cried out with pleasure as I let my head sink between her breasts.

Margaret

There was the sound of a door slamming and footsteps came towards us.

Nigel froze.

The door flew open and there, framed in the doorway was an irate woman.

She was tall, slim, dark and elegant – but, most of all, she was angry.

"It's true, then," she hissed. "You've brought another hussy home."

I grabbed for my top and quickly covered myself.

My face was burning. There was nowhere to hide.

Nigel stood and faced the newcomer. "Jemima," he blurted. "You weren't due back until tomorrow."

"Idiot!" she snapped. "You think I don't know what you're like. Get rid of that little tart at once."

"Who is this?" I stuttered, looking at Nigel for help.

"Who am I?" laughed Jemima, "Only his fiancée - if he thinks he can play around like this every time my back's turned he's got another think coming!"

"I'm sorry," I said. "I'll leave."

I wanted to pick up my belongings and looked longingly at the record player but didn't dare go towards it. My coat was in the hallway. Jemima must have seen it as soon as she arrived.

I felt dizzy and about to burst into tears. Getting dressed in front of this woman was about as embarrassing as anything could be.

"Jemima-I can explain," Nigel was muttering. Somehow he didn't seem quite so in control.

Jemima held the door open for me. "Just keep away from him in future," she snarled.

I scuttled down the stairs and out into the night. Now what was I to do?

Was it too late for buses – or should I look for an underground station? I only had a vague idea of where was. I knew my home was west of here – but which way was west? It had taken fifteen minutes by car. How far was that?

Chiswick, I remembered. I am in Chiswick. If I walked in one direction for long enough I'd find a shop, or a main road, or the river. Any of these would help me find my way home.

I was lucky. The underground was quite near and the

31

shop was only five minutes from my local station – but what could I tell my parents? It was only nine thirty. They would still be up.

I'd be as quiet as possible returning to my room but I'd probably be discovered.

I began to shake and the tears flowed freely. He'd been so charming and I'd been so gullible! What a fool I'd been. I'd never be able to go near him again.

Jemima had a key to his flat. She probably already lived there. She looked much more like his type of woman.

I felt humiliated. I wouldn't tell anyone what had happened. I would forget men and concentrate on my new job. I had a place of my own to find and I'd try again in the morning.

I didn't expect the estate agent to be open on a Sunday but I did want to walk round the area near the school and get a feel for the type of properties available.

According to the local paper, prices ranged from five pounds a week for a room to fifteen for a flat.

I couldn't afford a flat but would consider a bed sit so I bought a street map and began to explore.

There was something very satisfying about searching for somewhere to live. For the first time since I left college I felt in charge of my own life.

I would ring Tamsin and Georgie once I was settled. There was no room in my life now for the complications of a romance.

Graham

I put the shoe shop report to the bottom of the pile but by October I could no longer hide it. First, I thought, I'll revisit them and see what improvements have been made.

There were no customers in the shop and a portly lady who I guessed was Margaret's mother was alone at the desk by the till. She appeared to be counting tins of shoe polish and I waited until she stopped and looked up.

"Mrs Jones?" I enquired.

"Yes. Can I help you?"

"I'm Graham Harris. I expect your husband told you about my previous visit. You do seem to have made some changes."

"Yes, but having the boxes up to the ceiling makes it difficult for me," she replied.

"Your daughter is not at home?"

"No, she doesn't get in until after five on weekdays. She's a teacher, you know."

"Yes, I just came to find out if she was still occupying the stock room."

"Not for much longer, I believe. She spends every weekend looking at bed sits."

Mrs Jones looked angry and I didn't know quite how to respond.

"Well, perhaps you'll let me know when the changes take place," I said, trying to sound conciliatory.

"I'll tell her," snapped Mrs Jones. "I expect it will be after half term."

I felt dismissed. I was a fool not to have gone at the weekend. Hopefully I would get a better reaction from

Meg. For some reason she had stayed in my mind and I wanted to find out more about her.

What an idiot I was. I should have tried to discover where she worked.

I hadn't had much to do with girls. My sister's friends bored me. I'd rather go hiking over the hills than jig about at night clubs. Women and peace didn't seem to go together and I enjoyed the latter.

Now I had to go and check on a basement that had rats. At least I was doing something useful for society.

2

HOPE

Margaret

The last period had been art and packing up had been chaotic and noisy.

I wanted to go straight home but I had a prospective flatlet to view and it was in an attractive street only five minutes from the school. There was a corner shop and a bus stop nearby and if it turned out to be clean I meant to take it. I'd be sharing a bathroom but it had its own tiny kitchen and toilet – more than most of the other rooms I had seen.

I fell in love with the place on sight. It was light and airy and the furnishings were solid and attractive. The carpet was a little worn in places but I could hide that with a mat.

I had a feeling the woodwork had just been polished because the room had a sharp, lavender smell.

"I'd like to take it," I told the landlady. "How much deposit would you need?"

"A month in advance and an extra week's money in case of damage. That's returnable when you leave, if everything is satisfactory."

I've been saving, I thought, but it won't leave me much.

"Can I move in next week?" I asked. "I have five days off."

"Of course. You will be bringing your own bed linen and towels, I suppose."

"Yes. I'll bring some from home to start with."

"If you need to change anything – the curtains for instance, please ask me first."

"Certainly. I can bring a radio, can't I?"

"Yes, but nothing too noisy. The other residents play music but they don't seem to disturb each other."

I hadn't considered the other residents. Of course, the house had four floors and this was the first floor. I must have someone above and someone below me. I hoped they would be friendly.

Going home on the bus I hugged the thought of my new home to me. How relieved my father would be that he could tell that obnoxious young man that they would be using the stock room again.

By early October I had settled into my new flat and was enjoying my job.

One of the other teachers had invited me to a party. "I hope you aren't easily shocked," she said. "It's a pyjama party."

I can't go in my old pyjamas, I thought – but there was something I could do. I could make some pyjamas, shortie pyjamas. I'd seen some in a department store and I was sure I could sew a set in time.

It seemed daring and exciting – and it was a long time since I had done anything like that.

I knew a few of the people who would be there – so it wasn't quite so embarrassing as it could have been, but I arrived late on purpose – ready to take flight if it looked like an orgy.

The owner of the house let me in and I peeped into the living room. Music was playing, softly, but most people were chatting. It looked very civilised for a pyjama party. Perhaps the very fact that they were in night clothes made people more inhibited.

Leaving my coat in the hall I went into the kitchen for a drink. As usual, I had brought a bottle. It was the only way to ensure there was something I liked to drink. There were plenty of cans – and a bowl of punch on the kitchen table.

I looked round for a bottle opener.

"Here," came a voice from behind me. "Is this what you're looking for?"

I know that voice, I thought. It's Graham Harris. What's he doing here?. I tried not to show my displeasure and, instead, gave him a grateful smile as I turned to accept the proffered bottle opener.

"Hallo, Graham."

"Hey, it's you. What a fetching outfit." He grinned.

"You're well covered up, I see." I sneered, looking at the blue and white striped cotton pyjamas with covered buttons that hung on him, making him look like a fugitive from a Dickens novel.

"Don't have any jimjams – had to borrow my dad's. You want a hand with that?"

"Thanks. I released the bottle of white wine I had

brought with me and he opened it.

"Did you have it in the fridge?" he asked. "It seems quite cold."

"Yes. I wonder if I could hide it in one here?"

"Not all of it," he replied and poured out a large glass and handed it to me.

True enough, there was no room in the fridge but there was an ice bucket with an empty bottle of champagne in it. Graham replaced it with my bottle of wine.

"Don't expect it to be here when you come back," he laughed.

"What are you drinking?" I asked.

"I'm trying to make one can of beer last all night but I'm losing the battle. I've got to drive home after this. Shall we go in?"

I didn't like the way he seemed to have adopted me but I acquiesced. I supposed it might be the easiest way to get rid of him.

The seats had been pushed back against the walls and a few people were slow dancing to the music in the middle of the floor.

I took a sip of my drink and looked for the hostess. She seemed to be in a serious discussion with a bespectacled young man. I didn't feel inclined to intrude.

"Would you like to dance?" asked Graham. How was I ever going to get away from him?

"There's not room," I said, but I did set my glass down on the nearest surface. Why didn't my body do as my mind dictated?

Graham held out his arms ready to hold me and I nearly laughed out loud.

He looked like an overgrown schoolboy, standing there in his father's old fashioned pyjamas. His arms were long and thin and his hands looked too big and yet too delicate to belong to a man.

I stepped towards him and ducked my head into his chest to hide my amusement.

Taking my hand, he put his other arm in the small of my back and rested his cheek against my hair.

I felt him move to the music and began to relax. It was a comforting feeling – swaying together to a tune I liked.

"I'm glad you're here," he said, when the music ended. "I was ready to leave – but I thought Jonathan might want a lift."

"Is that who invited you?" I asked.

"Yes. He's a member of our walking group – but I think he's staying the night."

"Where do you go walking?"

"All over. Up Box Hill, on the North Downs, along the coast. There's a different walk every Sunday. I don't suppose you'd like to join us?"

"Where do you set off from?"

"Usually a railway station. We've got a programme. I think next week it's Sevenoaks – but I could pick you up."

It would be a change, I thought. Now the cricket's over I could do with getting out in the fresh air at the weekends.

"What time do you get back?"

"Not late. We stop at a pub for lunch and we're usually back by three. I'd love it if you could come – even if it's just until the cold weather."

"I'm not a softie!" I retorted. Did he think I was a complete wimp? "If I join I'll come in all weathers."

"I'm sorry. I didn't mean...." His voice tailed off. He looked chastened, almost timid.

I remembered, then, how we had first met. He'd almost chased me out of my own home, hadn't he?

"How's the shop?" he asked, almost as if he could read my mind.

"Fine – no thanks to you. Dad's put in a children's corner with some games and picture books.

"I've found somewhere to live – not as central, but near the school." Why did I tell him that? I didn't really want to see him again, did I?

I was angry at myself for enjoying the dance so much. How could I have been carried away by such a string-bean of a man – and one who seemed to have no social graces?

Still, if he was going to introduce me to a new activity and new friends, perhaps I would take him up on his offer.

Graham

I sensed her mood had changed and stood feeling helpless as she turned away as if she no longer wished to talk to me.

I couldn't think how to retrieve the situation so I finished my beer and made for the door.

"Going already, buddy?" called my friend.

"Yes, things to do – people to see," I responded, searching the crowd for Margaret to say goodbye. I couldn't see her, but I'd promised her a programme. I went out to the van and found what I was looking for.

When I turned round she was standing not two feet away.

"You're going, then?" she said.

"Yes. I just came out to fetch this for you. If you aren't at the shop I don't know where to find you."

"I know. That's why I wrote it down – here. Sunday morning, about ten?"

I took the note she handed me. Now I felt it was worthwhile coming to the party. She might be annoying but I wanted to get to know her better.

"Can I drop you anywhere now?" I said.

"No thanks. I'll see you on Sunday." It was almost a dismissal. I hoped she would be more friendly next time we met.

Margaret

When ten o'clock Sunday morning came and there was no sign of Graham's van I sat on the bed and removed my walking shoes.

We hadn't discussed phone numbers because I considered the one in the hall was just for emergencies.

By ten thirty I was fuming – fancy being stood up by a wimpy streak – after he had made it seem so important!

There was a ring at the doorbell, then another. Someone had urgent news. If it was Graham he needn't bother. I was in no mood for excuses.

Someone must have let him in because when I opened the door of the flat he was red faced and puffing as he came up the stairs.

"Sorry," he gasped. "The van broke down and I had to get it fixed. I need it for work – but finding someone on a Sunday wasn't easy."

"Is it OK now?" I asked, stepping aside to let him in.

41

"No. It will be off the road for at least two days. I'll have to use the bus, or take time off."

"Surely your boss will understand?"

"I expect they'll say it is my fault. I'm not supposed to use it for private trips."

"So what will you do?"

"Now, you mean?"

"No- next week?"

"I can't think." He sat down heavily on a kitchen chair. "Any chance of a drink of water?"

"Of course. I suppose we've missed the walk," I said, filling a glass from the tap and handing it to him.

He swallowed the lot. "Yes, but nothing's stopping us from going for one on our own. Do you know the area?"

"No, I don't, but there's a park behind the school, with a little zoo. It's quite extensive. We could go there."

His breathing seemed more controlled. "I ran," he explained. "All the way from the garage. I didn't want to be late."

I couldn't stay cross with him. Instead I opened the fridge and took out butter and cheese, tomatoes and lettuce. I reached into the larder for a loaf of bread. "I'll make us some sandwiches," I said. "We can go when you're ready."

Graham

I didn't like to tell her I didn't usually eat white bread. I wanted to make it up to her for spoiling her day.

I could see she'd dressed appropriately for the trip and had even tied back her brown curls into a pony tail which showed off her eyes.

Seeing her in a domestic setting made me like her more. I almost felt reluctant to go out. I'd like to have stayed there, just the two of us, with nothing else to consider but each other.

She broke the spell by filling a thermos with hot coffee and turned back to me proudly, announcing, "There. How's that for a picnic?"

I just stopped myself from replying, "Great, Miss." Instead, I took the bag she was holding and added it to my own pack.

"Good idea," I said, "Lead on McDuff."

Hearing her laugh made me feel good. I was going to enjoy the rest of the day.

Margaret

I couldn't remember the last time I had felt so relaxed.

It was like finding a long lost brother, I thought. Graham seemed to guess what I was thinking before I spoke and even if we disagreed we seemed to listen to each other – as if it was more important to understand than win an argument.

I found out that he preferred brown bread and that he lived at home with his parents and his sister. He had struggled at school until his final year when his form tutor had encouraged him and given him the confidence to pass exams.

"He told me to apply to the council," he said. "I started off as a clerk – but I went to night school."

"Do you like your job?" I asked.

"Parts of it, but I'd rather be a forest ranger, only there's not so many of those jobs going."

"There's not much forest round here."

"I don't care where I go. I'd like to travel."

"Flying scares me – but I guess if I wanted to go somewhere hot for a holiday I'd give it a go."

We had reached the pen with the guinea pigs and were standing close together, watching them. I loved all the different colours, from bright ginger to black and white patched, some smooth and some with whorls of fine hair making them look extra comical.

"Some people eat them, you know," said Graham.

"Oh, no. They are so sweet. When I have a house of my own I'm going to have lots of pets."

We found a bench for our picnic and then followed the marked nature trail, reading the names of the plants as we went.

"This would be a great place to bring my class," I said. "There's so much here – look – a squirrel."

"A few children would be enough," said Graham. "If we are quiet we'll see the birds."

I had never known a man who was interested in birds of the feathered kind. I stood still, listening.

Without a word, Graham drew me to one side, where a gap in the trees looked out onto a distant view. We were on the crest of the hill. The parkland sloped down to a number of allotments and a canal and beyond them the railway line and the houses and factories of the town.

"I like being up high," I said.

"I like being with you."

"Do you mean that, Graham?"

He turned towards me. "Of course. You don't jabber and complain. You are a comfortable person to be with."

"Oh," I felt deflated. I'd never been called comfortable before. It wasn't exactly what I'd hoped to hear. But, there again, he wasn't exactly Tarzan, was he? Perhaps 'comfortable' was how he made me feel – or could there be the promise of something else?

He was a mystery I wanted to discover. I wanted to listen to him, understand him and make him laugh. He made me feel as if anything was possible. "Medicine," I muttered. "You are like medicine."

He did laugh, then, a deep throaty chuckle, and reached round to give me a hug.

"So are you," he said. "Perhaps we'll be good for each other."

We held hands as we walked back through the park. I wondered when I would se him again.

Next weekend I'd promised to help in the shop.

"There's a canal walk on Sunday," said Graham when we got back to the flat. "Can I pick you up at eleven?"

"Yes, please," I replied. "Maybe I'll meet your friends this time."

"I think today was better," he said, "but I must catch my bus. Thanks, Meg."

He gave me a brief peck on the cheek and left. The house phone was ringing in the hall and as no -one else was around I answered it. It was my mother.

"Your friend Tamsin rang," she said. "She gave me her number. Can you call her back? I think she wants to see you."

Tamsin

When I realised Georgie was going home for a few days at half term I was relieved. Living with her had not been as easy as I had expected. We were so different.

Luckily she was out more than I was, so I could spread out in the lounge and draw and construct as much as I liked, as long as I cleared it away before she came back.

She adopted the little third bedroom as a 'quiet space' as I liked music on when I was planning lessons. It wasn't the kind of music she enjoyed. She was into orchestral and operatic music which I found irritating.

Also, our tastes in food were completely opposite.

I didn't care much what I ate and was ready to try anything new, exotic or spicy.

Georgie like classic English cooking and insisted on a roast dinner at weekends.

We had a shelf each in the fridge, mine with ready meals and hers with eggs, meat and fish.

Once Georgie had left I rang Meg's shop.

Her mother answered and told me about Meg's flat, and that, although it had a phone, Meg didn't consider it hers because it was downstairs. She promised to try it and, some time later, Meg responded.

"Can you come over at the weekend?" I asked. "It's not hard to find, quite near the station."

"How about Saturday?" she replied. "I'm busy on Sunday."

"Super. Let me know when your train gets in and I'll meet you. Don't expect a palace. Our place is pretty grotty."

"It will be good to see you. Will Georgie be there?"

"No. She's gone back to the family pile. She was looking forward to riding her horse and catching up with the County set."

"She doesn't hunt, does she?"

"Goodness knows. She doesn't talk to me much."

"I'm sorry, Tamsin. Never mind. I've got a lot to tell you."

"Great. See you Saturday. Bye."

Everyone seemed to be having a more exciting time than I was. I needed to get out in the evenings and see what was going on.

There was a funfair in town. Maybe that would be interesting. Meanwhile I had to decide what to do with Meg.

Would she prefer somewhere historic, like Rochester, or somewhere quirky, like Horrid Hill?

I don't suppose she'd fancy shopping in Chatham, although there were a few nice places to eat.

Now I had to sort out the scraps of material I had collected for the hand puppets my class were going to make for Christmas. The papier mache heads were drying in the classroom cupboard – just waiting for their costumes.

Margaret

The visit to Tamsin was a rare treat. Father had said they could manage without me for once. The October weather was fine and sunny. The train journey was restful – no commuters on a Saturday and I was going in the opposite direction to people going to London for the day.

When Tamsin gave me the choice of what to do I opted for the walk by the river Medway.

She called the place we went to 'Horrid Hill.' I supposed it was horrid because of the slurping mud with air bubbles coming up to the surface which made a curious belching sound as if the place was alive. We had to take a narrow path onto a finger like peninsular, passing, as we went, a concrete boat settled into the mud. The walkway was bordered by bushes, laden with berries and ended in a point where we could look out over the water.

Graham would have loved it.

"I didn't bring a camera," I grumbled. " I didn't realise we'd be doing something like this."

"It's a fabulous place, isn't it? said Tamsin. "Now let's find a pub for lunch and you can fill me in on all the gossip."

"I wish I'd been like you," I said at last when we were seated in the pub. "I was too romantic. I thought I'd found the ideal man."

"Humph. There's no such thing."

"I found that out the hard way," and I told her about Nigel and his fiancée.

"You should look for someone more like you," she said.

"Stupid and naïve, you mean?"

"No. Natural and sympathetic. Someone honest."

"I think I may have met someone like that – but we got off to a bad start and I'm not sure how he feels about me."

"What's he like?"

"Thin, quiet, funny – not at all the sort of man you'd go for."

"He sounds boring. You know I like musicians and actors – creative people."

"But none of them lasted very long, did they?"

"They didn't have to. I like a change."

"And Georgie? What's her love life like?"

"Secret. She's more interested in becoming famous. She's signed up with a model agency."

"But she's still teaching?"

"Oh yes. You should have seen her face when they put her picture in the paper as the coach of the local netball team."

We finished our meal of chicken and chips and headed back to the house where Tamsin showed me the art work she had been doing with her class.

"Now you'll have to come and see my flat," I said. "Please keep in touch."

"Expect me at Christmas," she replied. "I'll be shopping in London and it's nice and near."

But by Christmas Tamsin had vanished.

Graham

I didn't really know what was happening to me.

I felt slightly detached from work – as if I were marking time – not completely involved.

I used to worry about my decisions when I got home and try to follow up every visit to make sure it was satisfactory, even if it meant doing it in my own time.

I became involved with the lives of the folk I inspected

-well, not all of them, of course, but the ones who struggled to conform to the regulations.

Now, nothing about my working life seemed important, I just waited for Sundays, when I could see Meg.

The time with her had a brightness, a sharpness, an immediacy that made me want to record every second so that I could replay it in my memory.

She'd made my weekdays dull in comparison. I thought I'd like her to be in my life all the time – but I didn't know how to tell her.

She seemed so content with her life as it was, I didn't want to spoil it.

Also, I had a feeling she was earning more than I was. She was making me confused.

Sometimes I felt like her friend and protector – she was almost a foot shorter than I was– and at other times she treated me like a schoolboy.

Sometimes I thought she was feminine and vulnerable and other times she was authoritative and dynamic.

Sometimes I could see she was listening and absorbing all I was saying and other times she seemed to be thinking about something else.

There is a current that runs through me when I hold her hand that makes me feel we belong together, but I don't know if she feels the same.

Sunday didn't help.

The walk along the canal was aborted because of a deluge of rain and we all took shelter in the pub. When we all crowded round a long table the conversation turned to November 5th and fireworks.

Some people wanted to go to the local organised display while others agreed it was a waste of money and frightened their pets.

Meg argued forcibly that children should be allowed to enjoy fireworks but that they didn't have to be so loud that it was impossible to keep animals calm.

"You can give them tranquillisers," I said, "but I would do away with fireworks altogether. Too many people get hurt."

"But it makes our history come alive," she argued. "Without events like this how do children learn from the past?"

"It isn't the children I'm concerned about. It's the stupid older people who don't know how to store them and the idiots who think it's fun to throw them around."

As soon as I had spoken I knew I had said the wrong thing. Of course I cared about the children but I was trying to emphasise that the problem lay with the fireworks and, that if they didn't exist, no-one would come to harm. It was part of my job to inspect the storage facilities for dangerous items like fireworks but I had no control over what people did once they were purchased. I was thinking as if I was on duty.

I didn't get a chance to explain

Meg ate her ploughman's in silence and then asked abruptly to be taken home.

"You'll come again?" I asked, hopefully.

"Perhaps," she said. "If the weather's better – but I'm very busy."

I didn't want her to go.

She looked flushed as she let herself out of the passenger door of the van.

"Meg," I called out as she passed me. "Can I take you for a meal, to make up for today?"

"I don't know. Wait for the holidays. It's a bit hectic at the moment. I've got the programme. If I want to join a walk I'll ring them."

I was choked. I watched as she let herself into the house and felt as if she was walking out of my life for ever.

What had gone wrong? We had been getting on so well. Had I misjudged her feelings? Was she just using me to find new companions?

I drove away, disconsolate.

Margaret

How could I? How could I begin to fall in love with a man who preferred animals to children?

I'd been a fool again – projecting my image of an ideal partner on someone entirely unsuitable – just because he was different from Nigel. I hadn't really expected Bob to be a long time partner but I did long to be a wife and mother and I had invested a lot in my dreams of a future with Nigel. Now, I realised, Graham had been a rebound and I had recognised it just in time.

As I calmed down I began to wonder if I could still keep him as a friend, even if he didn't care for children. We would just have to agree to disagree. Our relationship could never go further.

For now, work took up nearly all my time and I spent each Saturday in the shop, dressing the windows with decorations and a display of slippers and wrapping parcels in shiny coloured paper.

We had a tiny silver tree in the corner of the shop and a bowl of sweets for the children.

Mum and Dad put a real Christmas tree upstairs and I stayed overnight at the weekends, writing cards and watching TV. It was cosy, but I was missing Graham. I hadn't even got his address and I didn't dare ask the Council.

He knew where I lived. If he wanted to get in touch it would be easy. If he didn't, I'd know he had just seen me as an interlude.

I didn't go on any more walks.

Tamsin

It started with the Haunted House.

When Meg had gone back it was still early in the evening so I went in search of the funfair.

The big wheel was lit with a circle of bright lights and organ music came from the rides.

A tall, muscular man invited me to try the 'Test Your Strength,' but I declined and walked on to the Magic Mirrors and the Haunted House.

Some of the light bulbs on the wooden buildings were out and even in the dark I could see the paintings on the outside were pale and shabby.

This was an amusement that had seen better days.

I paid my shilling and climbed into the wooden seat. When a few more people joined me we set off along the track.

I'd been in such tunnels before and knew what to expect, spider's webs, skeletons, grotesque faces, bloodied hands coming from nowhere and horrific squeals and moans.

However, the carriages clattered and creaked along

the track and some of the 'horrors' looked decidedly decrepit.

The children in the seat behind me seemed satisfied but I was determined to come back in daylight and see how bad the problem really was.

On Sunday I worked on my lesson plans in the morning, had a quick lunch of soup and toast and then returned to the fairground.

It looked different in the day – some of the stalls were empty; children and dogs were running around and there was the sound of hammering from behind a caravan. The only thing that looked brand new and shiny was the bumper cars.

The bright vehicles were newly painted and the floor had a polished look. The poles were smooth and the rails gleamed in the sunlight. If only all the rides had looked like that one.

When I reached the haunted house it was even worse than I remembered. The figures on the front had once been witches, dragons, snakes, spiders and a terrifying executioner with a bloodied axe. There may have been a head at his feet but the wooden wall had been worn away and the track inside was visible through the rotten timbers.

"What you doing here?" asked a stout woman behind me.

"Just looking," I replied. "I wondered if I could help."

"We aint taking on newcomers," she snapped. "You're not travelling kind, are you?"

"No – but I'm willing to work for a couple of weeks – if you'd have me. I like painting."

"S'pose it won't do no 'arm. You'll need to see Mike. I'll show you."

She shuffled through the site to a large caravan and knocked on the door.

"Mike – you there?" she called.

"Sally? What's up?"

The man who came to the door was short, bearded and wearing a vest and shorts.

"This 'ere woman wants to paint," she replied. "I'll leave you to it," and she moved away.

"Paint what?" he asked, puzzled.

"I'm sorry. My name's Tamsin. I really like your rides but I wondered if you'd let me go over some of the art work on the front. It looks pretty worn."

"It's original," he said, "but I suppose it does look old, especially against the bumper cars. How much would you charge?"

"I'd do it for nothing," I said, recklessly, "as long as you provided the paint, and gave me a free hand."

"What does that mean?"

"Well – I'd run my designs past you, of course, but some of the drawings need updating."

"Tell you what. You do some pictures of what you mean by a makeover. We are here until Tuesday – then we go to Sussex for a break. That's when we sort out problems and smarten everything up. Could you come with us?"

It would be the Christmas holidays. I could manage a couple of weeks – but would that be enough? It was too tempting an offer to refuse.

"Yes. There's nothing to keep me here. I'll bring some ideas tonight."

I would have to work fast but I already knew what I wanted to do. The trouble was, the images I wanted to portray could mean there had to be changes made inside as well. I'd deal with that if I got approval.

"I'm on the shooting gallery," said Mike. "See you tonight."

I did a few sketches that afternoon, brightening up the skeleton, making it more active and cartoon looking, and I added a robot and an octopus. I did a classic ghost and an especially frightening witch – her long green face with snarling white teeth and her black cloak flying out behind her as she rode her broomstick. I changed the spider, too, making it more hairy, with big googly eyes.

I took the pictures to the caravan that evening, as soon as the fair had closed, and found there were three other people there with Mike.

The man from the ' Try Your Strength' game and two women I had not seen before,leaned on the table as I passed round the pictures.

The younger woman looked impressed. "Hey, these are good," she said. "Imagine how much better the place would look with these colours."

"Would you paint them yourself?" asked the man.

"Sure – if you gave me the paint and a ladder," I replied. I didn't like the sneer in his voice.

"What do you think, Mike?" asked the other woman.

"When could you do it?" he asked, turning to me.

"In these Christmas holidays. I'm an art teacher."

"We wouldn't be indoors," said the man.

"I realise that," I snapped. "I'd come to wherever you were."

"You could bed down in my van," said the young woman.

"We'll be at Nuttington from the tenth of December," said Mike. "Give me a list of what you want and we'll have it ready. OK, Vince?"

Vince nodded in agreement and then got up and left. The others seemed to relax.

"Let's have a drink," said Mike. "If you make a good job of the haunted house perhaps we can find you some more to do."

"Vince is supposed to be in charge of maintenance," explained the young woman. " He feels guilty that he's let the interior get so shabby. I'm Sue and this is Jenny."

"Pleased to meet you," I said, belatedly.

"I bet he'll have it tidied up by the time you join us," said Jenny.

"That won't be until the end of term," I said. "He'll have plenty of time."

Once the Christmas parties were over I packed some things and, leaving a note for Georgie, set off for the South Downs and Nuttington.

I still couldn't drive but I had a bicycle and, rather than taking the train in and out of London, I decided to make it an adventure and ride across country.

Did I know, then, that I would not be coming back?

Maybe I was wise enough to wait and see how it all turned out but the feeling of joy and freedom that I felt as I rode through the lanes was intoxicating. I was riding with hope – and leaving nothing behind that I treasured.

This Christmas would be very different from all those that had gone before.

Margaret

When I came out of school on the last day of term a white van was waiting on the corner.

I turned and walked in the opposite direction but he drew away from the kerb and followed me.

When he parked up beside me I stopped and rapped on the passenger window.

He bent over and opened it. "Want a lift, Miss?"

I looked behind me. There were no children in sight so I climbed in.

Graham looked happy. It was good to see him smiling and I realised I'd missed him – but I wasn't going to let him know.

"Are you checking up on me?" I challenged.

"In a way. I've got an invitation. Do you want to go straight home?"

"Of course. I'm tired and I have all this stuff to put away." I was sitting with a briefcase and a bulging carrier bag on my lap.

"I thought we could go for a cup of tea and a toasted teacake."

For some reason that seemed amusing, coming from him.

"You little old fashioned thing," I teased.

"Well?"

"OK. If you take me home straight after."

His eager expression made me smile.

The shopping centre was decorated for Christmas and as it was getting dark there were lights everywhere. I was on holiday. My time was my own for two whole weeks. I began to relax.

"What's this invitation, then?" I asked when we sat down.

"I'll tell you when we've ordered. I'm starving."

He sat opposite me and there was a sparkle in his eyes as he began, "The Council has a Christmas dinner dance every year in the Town Hall. This year it is next Saturday night. I need a partner. Can you come?"

"What kind of dinner dance?"

"Quite posh. Lounge suits are allowed but the women go to town with long frocks. Is it too much?"

"You think I don't have a long frock? I'm not posh enough for you?"

He began to stammer. "No – I don't know – I've only ever seen you in casual stuff. I'm making a mess of this, aren't I?"

He had such a hang -dog expression that I had to laugh.

"Don't be pathetic. I'd love to come. I don't have anything exciting planned for Christmas, although I did think I might go to a pantomime."

"How about I take you to the dance and you take me to the panto?" he said, cheering up.

"That's a deal. What time shall I expect you on Saturday.?"

"Six thirty? The invite is seven for seven thirty."

"I won't know anyone, will I?"

"The local MP will be there – but we won't be on his table."

"Is there a choice on the menu?"

"I think so. I didn't go last year. Thanks for saying yes."

He munched his teacake with renewed relish and I felt a surge of fondness towards him. There was a kind of boyish charm about him. It wasn't sexy – but it was pleasant.

I was looking forward to Saturday night.

He'd almost been right. I didn't own an evening dress.

I had a long black skirt and some fancy tops but they made me feel old.

I would have to buy something new.

Once at home I would ring Tamsin and tell her about my date. We hadn't spoken for weeks and I wondered what she was doing for Christmas.

But it wasn't Tamsin who answered the phone – it was Georgie.

"I'm glad you rang" she said. "Do you know where Tamsin is? She left a note telling me to turn off the central heating when I went home as she didn't know when she'd be back."

"I haven't a clue," I replied. "I was expecting to see her in the holidays."

"Well, she's gone somewhere – and left a month's rent. It's all very inconvenient."

"I don't think you need to worry," I said, "She's well able to look after herself. Has she met anyone new recently?"

"I don't know. We haven't been talking much. This living together doesn't seem to be working."

"She wouldn't go back to her mother's, would she?"

"Certainly not. She's told me often enough that she's never going to see either of them again."

"Then we'll just have to wait and see if she gets in

touch. Give me your home number and I'll let you know if she contacts me."

"Thanks, Meg. Are you all right?" "

"Fine, nothing new here," I said. She told me where she would be at Christmas and I sent greetings to her family.

Georgie was not the sort of friend you shared your dreams with. I would just have to go shopping on my own, or take my mother.

I decided I'd scout the department stores in Ealing before I ventured further afield.

As there would be politicians present I would steer away from red and blue. I would just try to find something that fitted – not easy with my shape.

But when I entered the second shop I changed my mind. There, on display, was a beautiful full skirted peacock blue dress, shimmering under the store lights.

It wasn't too revealing – it had a shaped neckline and tiny cap sleeves, a fitted bodice and the kind of skirt that makes a girl feel like a princess.

When I asked the assistant if I could try it on she looked me up and down and declared, "That one isn't in your size – but I could fetch one for you to try and perhaps we could shorten the hem."

I was terrified that I might be too fat. The material didn't look as if it would stretch – but when I put it on it fitted perfectly. As she had expected – it dragged on the floor.

Then she told me the price of the dress, and the alterations. It was twice what I had allowed for.

I stared at myself in the mirror. My hair looked

wrong. I would need a fortune for this one occasion. Was it worth it?

"The dance is next Saturday," I said. "Would it be finished in time?"

"The alterations could be done in 48 hours, once you had purchased the dress," she said. "It really does suit you."

It did – and I told myself I could wear it again. There would be other events. I would be ' The girl in the peacock blue dress.'

"I'll have it," I said and took out my cheque book. There wouldn't be much money left for Christmas presents but this was an investment – wasn't it?

The day of the dance I spent the morning in the shoe shop, trying to stifle my excitement.

I had a hair appointment in the afternoon and my hair was swept back and draped over one shoulder. I returned to my flat too nervous to have anything but a cup of tea.

I couldn't imagine that Graham would arrive in the van and was delighted when a taxi pulled up five minutes early.

I needed my duffle coat against the cold and I was glad it wasn't raining because I was wearing new high heeled shoes.

"Hi there, Cinderella," said Graham as he opened the door for me.

"Will I do?" I asked.

"I hardly recognised you," he replied.

It wasn't exactly a compliment.

* * *

The hall was decorated in red and green with a huge Christmas tree in one corner and green and red streamers and balloons hanging from the ceiling.

The circular tables sat eight and were covered with white cloths. At each place setting was a red mat, napkin and cracker and there was a table decoration in the centre made up of a candle, holly and red and gold baubles.

The waiters were placing bottles of red wine and ice buckets of white wine on the tables.

I had left my coat in the cloakroom and now had time to take a good look at my companion.

Graham was also in blue, a rich cobalt blue that made him stand out among the black and charcoal suits that most of the other menfolk wore.

His shirt was white and his tie had horizontal stripes of sky blue, green and white.

I looked up into his face. His eyes were blue, too, I thought, and he's not so gawky looking.

Then he smiled and my heart lurched. It wasn't a reaction I had expected.

"They're sitting down," he said, softly, taking my arm. "I've checked which table we're on, ready?"

Graham sat on my left and the rest of the table was made up of people from his office and from the parks department.

In fact I had met one of the women before, when I was trying to organise a trip out for my class to collect conkers.

Her husband sat between us and studied the menu with care.

"I'll have the beef wellington," he said. "We prefer red wine."

"What would you like, Meg?" asked Graham.

"The turkey, please, and prawn cocktail as a starter."

"I'll join you, but with the soup, and Christmas pudding to follow?"

"Perfect."

I was happy. There was no way I was going to drink red wine. I just hoped the helpings were fairly small if I was expected to dance afterwards.

Fortunately there was a pause after the meal for coffee and speeches, so by the time the band struck up I felt ready to take to the dance floor.

I had never danced properly with Graham, only smoochy dancing at the party, but he held me firmly and strode out in time to the music. I felt as if I was floating as my wide skirt swirled out and around me. I had thought he might tread on my toes but he seemed to be a different person, skilled and in control. He made me feel as if, together, we could do anything – and he made me feel as if I wanted to stay close to him for ever.

"You can dance!" I exclaimed as we sat down.

"And you're pretty light on your feet for a dumpling," he retorted.

"I can only waltz and quickstep," I said, "but I'd rather jive."

"You'll have to teach me. My sister made me take ballroom lessons. She said it was the only way I'd meet girls. She's exceptional."

Maybe it was the wine -but I found I didn't want to let him go – unless, of course, we were going home together. He was so different, so desirable. What was happening to me?

Graham

Once Meg was in my arms the rest of the room seemed to be a blur. I could hear the music, I could feel her arms on mine and her body so close that it was almost painful.

Did she guess how she made me feel?

Did she know how difficult it was to make polite conversation when all I wanted to do was to take her somewhere we could be alone and divest her of that bright blue dress? I wondered what she was wearing underneath and felt myself getting hot.

"I'll be back in a bit," I muttered and, untangling myself from her grasp, rushed out of the hall as quickly as I could.

I splashed my face in the cloakroom and then stood on the Town Hall steps – breathing in the cold night air.

Meg wasn't the kind of girl I could have a quick fling with. If I went on seeing her it was likely to get serious.

Was I ready for that? If not, I would have to find a way to let her down gently.

But could I do that – or should I let nature take its course and show her how I felt?

When I returned to the ballroom Meg was dancing with someone else.

I felt a mixture of relief and jealousy.

My colleague, Miriam, was sitting alone so I asked if she'd like to dance. She was stiff and kept her body some distance from me. When the tune ended I thanked her and looked for Meg.

She was seated at our table looking uncomfortable.

"Are you OK, Meg?" I asked.

"Just a bit tired," she said. "Would you mind if we went home?"

"No, of course not. Some people have gone already. I'll meet you in the lobby."

My blue belle had wilted – but I would be the perfect gentleman and escort her home.

Tamsin

Sue's caravan was warm and cosy.

I was tired and sore when I arrived at the camp site where the fair was to overwinter.

Although I was ready to bunk down with Sue I longed for a hot bath. I should have booked into a hotel for one night. Instead I curled up under a thick duvet on a narrow bunk and instantly fell asleep.

By morning the caravan was rocked by a severe gale. There was shouting and running footsteps from outside. I couldn't see through the tiny window as it was all misted up.

There was no sign of Sue and I needed to use the toilet. After a frantic search I found it just in time.

Once I was comfortable I found my shoes and coat and ventured outside to see if I could help.

Most of the caravans were still standing but one had tipped up and rolled down a slope.

The barn where the waltzer was stored had lost part of its roof and men were transferring equipment to the flat bed trucks at the entrance to the site. A loose tarpaulin flapped from the roof of the haunted house and Sue was trying to attach it to a nearby tree.

"We can't let it stay loose," she gasped. "It will smash up everything it comes in contact with."

"If I can climb up I can get it free," I called out. "Just hang on."

"Don't do that, you stupid bitch," came a shout as I reached up to haul myself onto the roof.

"It needs to be free," I yelled back.

"No, it doesn't. We need to reattach it."

Vince was carrying a long rope and a set of steps.

"Give me that end," he said to Sue and she released the side she was holding.

Immediately it blew upwards like a parachute but Vince held it tight.

Sue took the ladder from him and set it up against the wall of the haunted house at the opposite corner from where I was., crouched against the wind. I had pulled myself onto the roof and was trying to control the flapping material. The rain hammered at my face and my hands felt frozen, but I could see what Vince was trying to do.

The roof was open to the elements and only the tarpaulin could protect the inside from the storm.

Once he had secured his side he moved the ladder round to me and we made the rest fast.

At least one attraction was safe.

The runaway caravan had been righted and moved up the bank. People were retrieving bits and pieces that had been blown over but the storm was abating and everyone seemed calmer.

"My caravan for a pow-wow," shouted Mike and we trudged through the mud as directed.

As I reached the doorway I suddenly felt dizzy and began to fall.

Strong arms held me up and then I was lifted and taken inside the van.

Vince set me down gently and turned to Mike, "A drink of water, here," he said, "and then we can get something warm inside her."

Looking at me, he said, "When did you last eat?"

I blinked, still woozy and trying to focus.

"Yesterday," I said. "Breakfast."

"Good grief, woman, that's dangerous," he said.

"Coffee and toast all round," came Jenny's voice. "Mike, have you got any honey?"

There was a chorus of assent and I sat back against the seat. I wanted to go back to sleep. I didn't want to be interrogated and I didn't like the way Vince bossed me about.

I'd been a fool to come and the sooner I went back to my old life, the better.

The next day dawned crisp and bright. A weak winter sun shone on the camp. Puddles glistened and the air felt fresh and clean

I couldn't resist going to look at the haunted house to see the extent of the damage.

"You know what's missing," said a deep voice behind me - "Bats. I know people shouldn't be afraid of them, but they are - and if I hang some inside you can add some to the pictures on the front."

Vince was right – introducing bats would be a cheap and easy way to add to the horror level.

"I'm not going to paint over everything," I said. "I'm going to keep the executioner – it's part of history. Maybe if we make it less like a castle and more gothic we could put him in a window. I'd go over the paintwork, of course, so he was as bold as the new stuff."

"I'm glad you said that. I thought you'd want to turn it into a cartoon haunted house."

"Didn't Mike show you the drawings?"

"I didn't take much notice. It felt like a criticism – and now there's even more work to do, patching up the broken bits."

"Let me help," I said, looking at him properly for the first time. He reminded me of Robert Mitcham with his square shoulders and his half closed eyes. I couldn't help myself. I found him attractive.

"Let's find the executioner and see if we can agree on something," he said. "I guess you just want to paint over the rest, but I didn't know what colour."

"Grey, I think. The walls should be light grey. We could have dark clouds at the top and maybe flashes of lightening. I hadn't considered the background."

The wooden panel we were looking for was still in place, next to the entrance.

"It needs replacing," said Vince, "But the others look OK."

"If you can take it out I can restore it more easily," I said. "I'll need to keep the colour scheme, but it was drawn beautifully."

"I wouldn't exactly call it beautiful," he laughed. "How about some breakfast and then we'll get started."

His caravan was enormous. It looked American and his idea of breakfast was nearly as big.

He cut four doorsteps of bread from a white loaf, fried eight rashers of bacon and sandwiched them between the slices.

We washed it down with strong tea, two mugs each, and I felt ready for anything.

He was looking me over and I began to feel embarassed. "You need to grow your hair," he said at last. "It's almost as short as mine."

As his curled behind his ears that wasn't very short.

"You wanted to start," I said, and he laughed.

"Yes, while it's fine. I'll show you what we bought and you can tell me what else you need."

There were tins of white primer, which would do as a base coat and plenty of sandpaper and different sized brushes.

"If we take down the executioner I can put a frame round him and clean him up. The I'll try to match the colours they used originally. I'll use him to work out the sizes of the other windows."

The rest of the morning was spent assessing the damage and selecting the colours I needed.

In the afternoon Vince took me to the Cash and Carry and I found the grey, black, red, green and brown I wanted to start with.

By evening I was exhausted and made my way back to Sue's caravan. She had a warming hotpot on the stove and I had a quick wash and joined her for a meal.

"What are you doing tonight?" she asked.

"Vince wants me to take him the drawings. He said he'd not looked at them properly before."

"You do know he fancies you, don't you? He's very determined."

"I did feel something. He hasn't got a regular girl friend, has he?"

"Vince? He never has a regular anything. He's a danger to women. Don't say you haven't been warned."

But hearing that had made me more interested. I liked danger. I'd handled men like him before. He wouldn't be the only one to carve a notch on his bedpost.

I knocked on Vince's door at 8pm and he opened it with a can of beer in his hand.

"Beer?" he asked.

"Yes, thanks." I wondered if he would put it in a glass, but he didn't.

I sat at his table and opened the folder to show him the drawings.

He gave me a quizzical look and sat next to me, his arm draped casually across my shoulders.

I took a mouthful of beer and began to explain the drawings.

His fingers were tickling my neck and when I turned to question him he bent his head towards me and gave me an exploratory kiss.

I gave up pretending I didn't know what he wanted and returned his kiss.

He swiftly picked me up and dumped me onto his bed and began to strip.

I kicked off my shoes and took off my jeans – but had no time to do more before he had pushed me backwards, taking hold of my two wrists with one hand, wrenching them above my head, while pulling down my knickers with the other.

I wriggled, but my heart was beating fast and I wanted him to continue.

It wasn't tender, but it was fast and furious and made me feel like a captive slave girl. I had never felt such an exquisite orgasm.

I yelled. I couldn't help it – and he growled in response.

When he let go of me he was hardly breathing heavily but he had a triumphant grin on his face.

"You don't wear a bra," he chortled.

"Never have – not enough to worry about," I said, searching for my underwear.

"Take everything off," he commanded – so I did, first my socks, then my sweater and t-shirt.

He retrieved his boxers and sat looking at me, as if I was a statue, or a model.

"I think we're well matched," he said at last. "Stay the night."

I couldn't refuse – it was what I had longed for from the beginning.

Margaret

Unsurprisingly there were a couple of taxis waiting outside the Town Hall and we soon arrived back at the flat.

"Do you want to come up for a coffee?" I asked, although all I wanted was my bed.

"Not tonight, thanks," said Graham, "But I would

like to see you again before Christmas. Perhaps we could go out for a quiet meal – just the two of us?"

"That would be lovely." My eyes were stinging and my feet ached.

"Will you be at the shop on Saturday?" he asked.

"Yes. Where else would I be?"

"I'll see you then. Thanks for tonight."

"I liked it. I hope I didn't let you down."

"Oh, Meg – that's my line." He stood in front of me, hesitating.

I reached up and kissed him, briefly, and then hurried through the front door.

I sat on the bed and let my shoes drop to the floor. Had I been too forward? Dancing with him had seemed so natural. Did that mean I could get close to him whenever I liked?

Did I pity him, admire him or even love him a little?

He wanted to see me agan – and the thought made me hug myself with delight.

'Don't get your hopes up – you romantic,' I told myself. 'He hasn't made a move on you, has he? He probably thinks of you like another sister.'

I made up my mind I would find out by Christmas. I would not let myself be hurt by a man again.

Graham

I had to get advice from someone. I told my sister.

"I can't bear the thought of her being with someone else," I said.

"But do you want to wake up every morning and see her across the breakfast table?" she asked.

"Yes – that's exactly what I want."

"And what does she want?"

"I don't know."

"Well, you'd better find out – before you make a complete fool of yourself."

"Can you recommend a nice quiet restaurant?"

"For a proposal?"

"Not necessarily – for an intimate dinner."

"What food does she like?"

"I don't know - British?"

"Oh, Graham, you're useless. What does she look like and what does she do?"

"She's five foot four and curvy – with brown wavy hair and brown eyes. I think she's beautiful."

"What's her job?"

"She's a schoolteacher.." I stopped speaking because my sister gave a snort.

"Don't be like that," I said, "She teaches the young ones, she doesn't boss me."

"I'd like to meet her. Why don't you bring her home? Have lunch out, somewhere like a garden centre and then bring her round for tea. Ask Mum."

"I'm not sure. I'd told her dinner. Maybe I'll just take her to a country pub. Everywhere will be gearing up for Christmas – nowhere will be quiet."

"There's a new Chinese restaurant opened up in town. Ask her if she'd like that."

"I don't even know if I'd like it."

"Well, try it first, Dumbo. I'll come with you."

"Tonight?"

"You'd better make it tomorrow. You've probably got to book."

Tamsin

Whe I moved my stuff into Vince's caravan nobody seemed surprised.

We worked well together. He let me lead when it came to renovations and I was happy to do what he wanted in the bedroom.

He was a better cook than I was but I was tidier. I had to be, there was little enough storage space in the van.

Once we had obliterated all the old drawings and Vince had replaced the rotten wooden boards I began to draw the new walls, windows and turrets.

Each window had a different horror – all things that people would meet inside – the spider, the witch, the robot and the ghost. Bats flew all over the building and in the sky where stormy clouds were lit by flashes of yellow lightning.

I gave the windows and eerie misty blue background and made each monster as colourful as I dared.

The final touch, a life sized skeleton that beckoned the visitors inside, stood by the doorway in pure white with glowing eye sockets that even I found disconcerting.

"It's not too much, is it?" I asked Mike. "Not as long as it doesn't move," he replied. "You really have transformed the place."

"I love the bats," said Sue, "They look alive."

"Just wait until you see the ones Vince has inside," I said.

Vince had been repairing the track and repainting the carts. He'sd used luminous paint on the backs so that as they disappeared into the dark each could be seen by the one behind.

He was working on the lighting and sound systems, adding moans, hisses and cackles.

Seeing what I had designed had awakened a competitive spirit in him and he saw each improvement as a challenge.

"We need wind," he said, and he was right. "The front looks stormy but it's too still inside."

"How about a door that opens by itself and lets in a draught," I said. "It could creak. There's always creaking doors in horror films."

"Exactly. I'll work on it. It wouldn't have to lead anywhere."

That made me think. I'd been with the fair for over two weeks.

I had spent Christmas with them, eating, singing and getting drunk and now I would be expected back at school. But I no longer felt like a schoolteacher.

I was living a creative and passionate life. Every day was an adventure and I couldn't wait until we were on the road again and I could witness the public reaction to my efforts.

Somehow I would have to let Georgie know that I was not coming back and find a way to tell the school. I needed an excuse.

I would have to have an infectious illness. What would stop them looking for me? Should I go abroad? I didn't want them to know where I was.

The fairground folk already called me 'Tammy.' I felt like a different person and I wanted to cut all ties with the past.

Also, I needed money.

It was fine, at first, offering to work for bed and

board but my savings were depleted.

Mike had suggested I run a stall of my own and I was trying to think what to do – perhaps caricatures – in a tent, like the fortune teller.

I could hardly run away again. I suspected I was pregnant.

3

EXPERIENCE

Margaret

Georgie rang me and told me she had heard from Tamsin.

She told her she was in Ireland, and sick. She had a form of measles and couldn't mix with children. She'd informed the Education authority and would let us know when she was better.

"She'll not be teaching, then?" I said, stupidly.

"No. She didn't say what she was doing. It seems she went over there on holiday but got too ill to return."

"It seems a bit fishy to me. I bet there's a man involved."

"Well, if there is, she didn't say. I'm going to have a real job paying for this place on my own. I need a lodger."

"Sorry, I can't help. I'm quite settled here, and I've got a regular boyfriend."

"Oh, Meg, I'm so happy for you. What's he like?"

So I told her about Graham and about the Chinese

meal we had shared, where neither of us knew what to order and had to keep asking the waiter, who was very helpful and gave us some hot flannels to wipe our hands and suggested a Chinese lager to go with our meal.

It was exciting, romantic, exotic and wonderful and I had never felt so happy.

Then, afterwards, Graham had told me he wanted me to meet his family.

He didn't propose. He seemed unsure of how I felt about him.

I suppose I had been holding back a bit. I didn't want my body to dictate to my head – but really I couldn't imagine my life without him in it – so I said yes, I'd like to meet them and we opted for Boxing Day.

His Christmas present to me was a locket. I had been knitting him a jumper and finished it just in time to give it to him on Christmas Eve when he had arranged to meet me at the shop.

Mum and Dad had invited him to join us for a drink after dinner and, although we would rather have been alone, it seemed fair that he should share some of the festivities with us.

He brought Dad a bottle of whisky and gave Mum a poinsetttia.

He looked very relaxed to be with us – they were beginning to treat him as family.

Tamsin

Christmas morning was spent in bed.

When we got up the camp seemed unusually quiet.

"Where are all the children?" I asked Vince.

"Haven't you noticed – most of them have gone home. We don't just live in caravans, you know. Most of the families have houses."

"But you don't?"

"No. My father and mother were circus people. They died. My aunt has a house in the village which will be mine one day. I'll see her later."

He looked miserable and I didn't ask further.

We had arranged to have lunch in the local pub but it was an uncomfortable meal and Vince was drinking heavily.

This was not my idea of Christmas Day and when he staggered home and fell asleep I was relieved.

He woke in a foul mood and left the van without suggesting I accompany him, the present I had bought for him, a camera, discarded.

The next day Vince allowed me to draw his caricature.

I had been given a tent. The fortune teller had a new, larger, one and I had her 'cast off.'

"Why do people want drawings when they can have photographs?" said Vince.

He hadn't liked my image of him.

I had captured his slight air of menace and he thought that side of him was well hidden.

"A caricature emphasises aspects of a person. It shows how unique they are. It's supposed to be amusing. Most people find it funny."

"And they pay to be made fun of?" he said, determined to misunderstand.

I think he was jealous that I would no longer be dependent on him. I would have my own share of the collective income.

Mike had already arranged that any extra painting I did would be on a paid basis and I started by dying the tent bright blue.

All the designs on the material would be black and yellow and, this time, they would be cartoons. I would need to show how skilful I could be to encourage people to enter.

Of course I started by drawing all the people on the site. I said they need not pay me but some of them did, especially those who wanted copies to send to relatives.

I was content, it gave me a chance to try out chalks, pencil and pen and ink.

We were well into January when a new face appeared at the camp.

I had just finished painting the 'Hook a Duck' stall and was returning to our caravan when I heard a guitar.

A young man was sitting on the steps of Mike's van, playing and humming to himself.

When he saw me he broke into song.

I had to smile – it seemed so wistful. When he paused I applauded. "I haven't heard that before. What is it?"

"Something I wrote," he said. "Would you like another?"

I had been tired, and ready to go home, but I was intrigued. Who was this long haired stranger?

He was quite small and very thin. His face was long and pale and he wore leather trousers and a flowery shirt.

It was like looking at an incarnation of Puck, and his playing was magical.

I didn't really hear the words. I just let the tune take over my consciousness and sighed when it ended.

"I think you have a precious skill" I said, even to myself, sounding like a schoolteacher.

He laughed. "I don't know you," he said. "I'm Jake," and he held out a hand.

"Tammy," I answered, gripping it. It was warm and firm. "I'm the resident artist."

He laughed again, an easy, natural laugh. "That's a new one. Dad never told me."

"Mike's your father?"

"Yes. I'm around for a few days. Nice to meet you, Tammy."

I hadn't realised I had been standing rocking from one foot to the other. I must have seemed impatient to be gone.

"And you," I said- turning away. Vince would be waiting. He didn't like it when I was later than expected.

Margaret

On the Sunday the walking group were going down to the coast for a 'seaside stroll' and Graham wanted to join them.

It wasn't raining, but it was a grey, cloudy day and I would have preferred to stay in, relaxing, with him.

However, it turned out to be a jolly refreshing way to spend the day and the meal at the pub was accompanied by plenty of singing and banter.

I watched Graham carefully, knowing I was dependent on him driving me home, but he limited himself to a pint of cider.

The walk had taken us over cliffs and along the beach and I felt invigorated.

"They're a great bunch," I said as we drove home.

"Yes, good friends," he replied.

"What was that girl saying to you that made you go all serious?"

"Paula? She liked you." He was avoiding the question.

"She doesn't know me."

"But she knows how I feel about you." He slowed the car and pulled into the kerb.

"I love you. I'm miserable away from you. I want to be with you for ever."

His blue eyes were wide and worried, his face so sad that I just wanted to hold him close and kiss him. I had thought I was making him happy, but his feelings were much deeper.

"And you?" he asked, trembling.

"Oh, Graham. I don't deserve you. I didn't dare hope you felt like that."

"You didn't realise I was having such a job keeping my hands off you?"

"I thought we were comfortable together."

"And now?"

"Now I don't know what I think."

"Well, don't think. We'll go home and I'll show you."

He started the engine and my heart began to thump. Did he mean what I thought he meant – and was I ready? Was this the man I wanted to spend the rest of my life with and, if so, could we start today? I had until we got home to decide.

He was gentle, stopping every now and then to look at my face, as if to ask permission to continue.

When we were both naked in bed, our hands

exploring bodies he bent to kiss my breasts and I gasped in surprise at my own reaction.

"You're OK?" he asked and I wanted to laugh. OK didn't come near to how I felt. I wanted him so much I could swallow him whole.

"Yes," I said. "Hold me tight."

I did wonder, for a second, how he knew to coax me into readiness, but then the power of his love making took over and I cried out as he pulled away from me.

My legs were wet and he was shuddering and sobbing on top of me.

"Graham? What's wrong?" I asked.

"I couldn't stop," he said. "I thought I could, but I couldn't."

"I didn't want you to," I said.

"I know, but I didn't have anything with me."

"That's OK. I knew the risks. We can be careful next time."

He sat up, then, and stared at me as if he could hardly believe what I had said.

"You are wonderful. I'm so glad I found you," and he smiled.

I pulled him down next to me on the bed and covered us both with the sheet.

"Can I stay the night?" he said, at last.

"I hoped you'd say that," I replied. "It's nice having you here, next to me."

It felt right, somehow – more right than anything I had ever done before.

Graham

How could I have been so lucky – to find a girl like Meg?

I had been worrying for weeks if she would allow me to go further. She had seemed so self contained and happy with things the way they were – while she was driving me mad, I wanted her so much.

It was fine when we were in company – I could watch her, listen to her and be proud that she was with me – but when we were alone I found I sometimes stopped listening to what she was saying and just watched her lips move and her hair shine and longed to have her in my arms.

I didn't plan to seduce her that day, if that's what it was. It was just such a happy time and Paula had teased me by asking outright if we were 'an item.'

Once the idea of making our relationship permanent had entered my head I couldn't get rid of it.

I didn't want to spoil things. I didn't want to hurt Meg, but I needed to know if she felt the same. I couldn't bear it if she refused me.

She didn't. She responded even more readily than I had hoped and loving her was more intense and satisfying than I had imagined.

Then, at the last moment, I realised I could make her pregnant and it was up to me to avoid that.

I don't know how I managed to draw back in time but the shock of it brought tears to my eyes. I found myself weeping with a mixture of relief and frustration.

She calmed me by talking about 'the next time' and I immediately knew everything was going to be all right.

I also knew that this woman was to be my wife.

There was no way I would let her go. I would be with her for ever.

Tamsin

I didn't tell Vince I was expecting his baby but he must have guessed something had changed.

We still made love, but I wasn't so uninhibited as before and I felt he was getting bored with me.

We didn't have much in common, except sex, and we were beginning to argue about the other attractions.

He was working on the big wheel, which didn't need painting and I was trying to think how we could manage in the caravan with a baby.

He was drinking more, too, and not taking me with him because I no longer wanted to fill myself with alcohol.

Then, when he came home in the early hours and woke me, breathing fumes into my face and clawing at my nightshirt, I pushed him away and called him an 'inebriated prick.'

His face turned purple and he smashed me across the jaw. I could feel blood in my mouth and nearly swalllowed a loose tooth.

I curled into a ball as he rained blows on my back and I screamed for help.

There was a hammering on the van door and concerned voices outside.

Vince stopped at once, shook his head and sat staring at me as if he had no idea what he had done.

"It's all right," I called out, weakly.

"Vince? Are you there?" It was Mike.

Vince sat up straight. "Yes," he replied.

"Is Tammy OK?"

He stared at me again, shaking his head. "Please," he whispered. "I'm sorry."

"I'm fine," I shouted back. "There's no problem. We'll be quiet."

Vince smiled at me then – as I spat out the loose tooth and got up to wash out my mouth. My face ached. I would have a bruise in the morning. Would they really think it was over-active love making? I doubted it.

However, the footsteps went away and we were left by ourselves.

Vince did not come to bed. Instead he sat at the table in the dining area and rested his head on his arms.

I didn't sleep. I was wondering how I could have a child with this man.

Would he change if I told him? I feared not. In fact I was almost certain it would make him worse.

I would have to leave the camp before they even started their spring travels. I would have to find somewhere else to bring up my baby.

But next morning everything seemed different. I had slept for about two hours and Vince brought me cereal and coffee.

He'd had a shower and his long hair made him look like Samson.

He was full of apologies, and excuses.

"It's my aunt," he said, "She's threatening to leave her home to a distant cousin – because he's married. She says it should be passed on to a family. I really thought it would be mine one day."

"It could be," I blurted out. "I think we will be a family this year."

"Are you asking me to marry you?" he exclaimed.

"No. I'm telling you I'm pregnant. We are going to have a baby."

He sat down heavily on the bed and my coffee spilled into the tray.

"You're sure?"

"No. I've not done the tests or seen a doctor – but there are other signs." I didn't feel like elaborating.

Vince looked stunned – then a slow smile spread across his face. "That will make all the difference," he said. "They haven't got any kids. I always thought you were special."

It was satisfying to have made him so happy – but I had the feeling I had made the wrong choice. Maybe if I met this aunt I would find out if he really did have a violent temper or if it had just been that one time.

"You can't go to the doctor looking like that," he said. "Can I get you a pregnancy test kit – or shall I ask Sue?"

"Yes please, I'd like to see her," I replied, but I had the impression he was going to keep me hidden until my face healed, and I was right.

Margaret

Graham's family were delightful. His father worked on the railways and his mother was a dinner lady at a Primary school.

I liked her straight away and we were soon swapping school stories.

Graham's sister sat opposite us at the tea table, looking smug, as if she was the one who had brought us together.

Graham was different in his own home, very much the younger sibling – but, in spite of his sister's gentle teasing, the house seemed full of love. That was the sort of family I wished for.

When he took me back to my flat that night Graham said, "I'm going to talk to your father tomorrow."

"Why?"

"I want to ask him If I can marry you."

"But you haven't asked me yet? I might say no."

His face flushed with alarm and then he realised I was joking.

Slowly he got down on one knee and holding my hand recited, "Margaret Jones, would you do me the honour of being my wife?"

"Get up, you silly thing, of course I will," I chuckled, "but I'm sure you don't need to ask my dad."

"Oh yes, I do. I want everyone on my side," he quipped. "Now, are we going to bed or do I have to put you over my knee and spank you for giving me a fright?"

"You dare," I said, jumping out of the way. "Bags I first in the bathroom."

We planned to have the wedding in August but, before that, Graham insisted we try to find a bigger flat.

"i've got enough for a deposit," he said, "and with us both working we can afford one with two bedrooms and its own kitchen and bathroom."

"It's a big ask," I said, but I'd reckoned without my parents. Although mother didn't really approve of our situation, Dad immediately started making enquiries among his contacts in the business community and by the end of March had persuaded Graham and me to take a look at a maisonette in nearby Greenford.

"It's a bit noisy," he said, "as it's on a main road – but it's got all you asked for, and it's the upstairs one so you won't have people running about over your heads."

I couldn't walk to school but I had a plan. I would get myself a scooter. That would take me to and from school without being tied to the bus timetable.

When I told Graham he began to try to dissuade me – but when I told him I had found a little Vespa and had booked some lessons, he relented. I think, secretly, he was proud of my initiative.

Tamsin

Vince was taking me to see his elderly aunt.

I didn't know what to expect. It certainly wasn't the neat, modern bungalow in a quiet close that turned out to be our destination.

The front garden was paved, with large pots of evergreen plants arranged in a diamond pattern. In the centre was a fancy bird bath – one of those masquerading as a roman pillar, with a fairy reclining on the rim.

We entered the porch and Vince rang the bell. It chimed!

Then the door opened and his aunt stood there, a tall thin figure in black. Her slate-grey hair was tied back in a bun and her hooked nose made her look like a bird of prey.

The image lasted until she had taken us into the main room and seen us seated.

"So you are Vince's intended?" she said at last. "You're not from a travelling family are you? Have you got Irish blood in you?"

I didn't know how to reply. "I don't know," I muttered.

"Vince says you've got talent," she went on, "Show me."

"You mean-draw something?"

"Yes, me."

I looked at Vince, who had a strange smile on his face. Had he expected this?

He went to a large mahogany bureau and took out a pad of writing paper and a pen.

"These do?" he asked.

"It won't be very good," I muttered.

"I'll be the judge of that." she snapped.

She adopted a pose – stiff backed – with her hands folded in her lap, and stared fixedly over my shoulder.

"You'll have to relax, " I said, but Vince glared at me and thrust the pad into my hand. It seemed one did not tell his aunt she 'had to' do anything.

I could have done a caricature. She had all the makings of a dramatic raptor, or one of the witches I had designed for the haunted house, but I felt this was more important. I had to try to capture her the way she wanted to be portrayed. I had to try to please her.

"You can talk while I draw," I said. "Tell me what you used to do at the fair."

She blinked, as if that was quite unexpected and a gleam came into her dark eyes.

"I had two concessions – the shooting gallery and a sweet stall," she began. "I never liked sweets, myself, but we made a good profit on the bags of rock and marshmallows, mint humbugs and sugar mice."

Her face had softened a little while she spoke, which was good. I wanted to capture the feeling of pride she exuded, turning the strength of character into something positive, not aggressive.

"And Vince? What was he like as a youngster?"

The question was a mistake. There was a sudden tensing of her jaw. Her neck twitched as if it was trying to reject a memory.

"He was unlucky," she said at last and I could feel Vince relax beside me.

"Moving around did not suit him. It made it hard."

"But I got used to it, aunt," said Vince. "I was too young to understand."

He turned to me. "The children nowadays stay in one place for much of the year, at least between seven and eleven."

So that was why he wanted the house. He had been moved about so much when he was little he hadn't had time to form friendships, or even to get much of an education.

"Tammy was a schoolteacher," he said to his aunt. "I've got myself a brainbox."

A small smile flitted across the old woman's face but she said nothing. She seemed to be staring into the distance, or the past.

I finished the sketch and showed it to Vince.

"Why didn't you do me like that?" he whispered. "Show her."

His aunt turned towards us, trying not to show how eager she was to see her likeness.

"Vince-make some tea," she ordered and held out her hand for the drawing.

Vince rose obediently and went out of the room.

I handed her the drawing.

She looked at it without speaking.

Then she looked at me.

"Be careful," she said. "He's competitive. If you are too good he will try to spoil it."

I was astounded. I didn't know how to respond and sat silent until Vince brought the tea.

"Well, what do you think?" he asked.

"She's got one skill, I suppose – but goodness knows how useful that will be."

I might have imagined it – but I think I saw her wink at me.

"You'll have to sign it," she said. "I can't have anyone thinking it was done by someone else."

"Thank you," I replied. "It will be a pleasure."

Vince looked at me – puzzled by the change in the atmosphere since he left the room.

"Cracker?" he said, handing me a plate of biscuits. It sounded so funny I laughed out loud and the mood in the room changed again.

"Can I show Tammy the rest of the house?" he asked when we had finished our tea.

"Yes, but not my bedroom. The garden's the best part – show her the garden."

We went through the kitchen, which surprised me by being big enough to hold a small table and chairs, and out into the back garden.

The place was a wonderland. Even in winter it was magical and in the summer it must have been beautiful.

93

There were winding shrub-bordered paths, little seats, gnomes, a windmill, a pond, covered with netting, but perfect for fish and frogs and steps up to a miniature folly.

"It's like a fairy playground," I said.

"She never had kids," said Vince. "She's been on her own all her life. This is her baby."

I hadn't heard him speak with such softness before. I held his hand. There was something sad about him, some deep misery that I had not been able to address.

"Thanks for bringing me, Vince," I said.

"She wanted to meet you. I think she liked the portrait."

"Yes. I'm glad."

"I suppose she was a good subject."

"Yes." I could feel him tensing and thought I knew what he was thinking. "Most people don't sit still enough for an accurate drawing. You just picked the right person at the right time."

He straightened his shoulders at the praise. "I'll show you the rest," he said. "Come on."

The bathroom was clean and bright, with a shower instead of a bath.

"We could put the bath back," he said.

"Vince, stop it!"

His mouth closed and his eyes narrowed. "Don't tell me what to say," he growled. "If I think it, I'll say it."

"Sorry. It just seemed – impolite, in the circumstances."

"In the circumstances," he mocked. "Sometimes you sound like a real prude."

But we were back with his aunt and I tried not to show we had been arguing. "It's a lovely garden," I said. "It must be a lot of work."

She shot a glance at Vince. "Yes," she said, "but there are people who will do it for love."

"And three pounds a day," he snapped.

"You have your own work," she continued. "I understand that. How is the haunted house?"

"We'll take some pictures," I said, trying to lighten the mood. "We could bring them to show you, couldn't we, Vince?"

"I suppose," he said, "and it's time we got back there."

He reached for the tea tray and took it out into the kitchen. I heard him running the tap and washing up. He was obviously at home here.

"Be strong," said the old lady, enigmatically. "And thank you for the picture. You've made me look regal."

She was right – there was a look of Queen Victoria about the portrait.

I may have annoyed Vince but I had made one person a little happier.

The longer the pregnancy went on the more Vince became irritated by my presence.

He began to stay out overnight and often came home drunk in the early hours of the morning.

I couldn't wait until we were on the road, away from whatever influences were making him like this.

At the end of January we began to get ready to move.

We had one booking locally in February and then we were off round the South coast, from Portsmouth to Dover and up to Chatham in Kent.

Nobody mentioned a wedding and I was glad. If Vince was going to be so volatile I had no wish to be married to him.

Graham

The flat was perfect, except we had no garden to go with it. There were two good sized bedrooms and a kitchen/diner as well as the lounge and bathroom.

The best thing was the view from the back . We had playing fields behind us and then, in the distance, a little wood.

I wondered, then, if I should tell Meg what I had been planning. It seemed a bit premature. I'd only been volunteering at weekends, but I was about to apply to train as a forest ranger.

In the end I decided that the best place to tell Meg about it was in a forest, so I suggested we spend a week in the Forest of Dean in the Easter holidays.

"What a great idea," she said. " That's somewhere I've never been."

I booked a country cottage for the week after Easter and hoped she would understand. Our flat was rented. The only thing that would prevent us moving was her work. It was a pity there were no forests left in Middlesex.

"How long is the course?" she asked when I eventually broke the news.

"Two years, I think," I replied.

"So we'd have two more years at the flat?"

"Yes – and maybe longer. It depends where there was a vacant position."

"Where are the likely places?"

"Here, the New Forest, the Peak district, Northumberland - all over the country."

"So that's why you brought us here."

"I'm afraid so. I wanted you to feel how much quieter and healthier it is. I wanted you to experience the beauty and the calm."

"Well, I was calm until you broke the bombshell."

"What do you think?"

"I think I can see why you want to do it – but I'll need time to get used to the idea. Of course, as long as we were not out in the wilderness I could get a job anywhere."

"You are a wonderful woman," I exclaimed, hugging her tightly and planting kisses on her hair.

"Stop it – you softy. If you're going to turn me into a country wife we'd better get exploring. Come on."

She didn't look angry or disappointed. I was relieved. Now all I had to do was enrol on the course.

Tamsin

Once we were on the road Vince seemed a lot happier.

He still stayed out some nights but he tolerated my presence and talked quite civilly about the activities in the showground.

I had the impression he expected to leave me and the child in a house and be free to do what he liked, once the baby was born. Perhaps he thought I could live with his aunt.

I loved going to the different towns and drawing the customers.

I also worked on the posters advertising the fair and designed leaflets to take to local shops.

By the time we got back to northern Kent I was almost ready to drop in on Georgie and tell her my news but I made the mistake of drawing Jake.

In fact, I didn't only draw Jake – we spent a whole evening together. After I had finished his caricature he invited me to a folk club where he was playing.

It was a warm and lively bar and the entertainers were varied – with a great deal of audience participation.

Singing lifted my spirits and we were laughing together as we walked back to the van.

Unfortunately it was a night Vince had elected to stay home.

He opened the door when he heard us and his face took on a self-righteous scowl.

"What time do you call this?" he boomed.

"I was just escorting your good lady home," said Jake, trying to sound conciliatory.

Vince ignored him. "Where have you been?" he snarled, looking at me.

"Just to a folk club. Jake was singing. I didn't think you'd miss me," I replied.

"Get in here," he ordered. "And you keep away from her," he snapped at Jake.

Jake shrugged and turned away.

I followed Vince into the van. He'd been drinking. I could smell it on his breath and wondered how I could calm him down.

I couldn't.

He swung at me and knocked me sideways. Then he pulled me to my feet and hit me. His blows were aimed at my body and I tried to protect myself with my arms but I heard a sharp crack and realised something was broken.

"Stop, Vince, please stop. I've done nothing wrong," I whimpered, turning with my back to him.

He kicked out at my legs and I felt dizzy with pain. I was rolling on the floor, crying and screaming.

There was a sudden draught and I glimpsed people in the doorway. Then the world went black.

I was no longer pregnant.

The beating I had received had not only broken my arm but caused internal damage and I lost the baby.

I was in hospital and a doctor was asking if I had any relatives. Who could I turn to? Who would look after me now?

I could only think of one friend – Meg. Surely Meg would help me. She was the least judgemental person I knew and her shop was the one address I could remember.

"Mr and Mrs Jones," I said and gave him their number. "Tell them it's Margaret's friend. If I can stay with her for a few days I'm sure I'll soon be better."

Margaret

My mother rang the new flat.

"I've had a peculiar call from a doctor in Gravesend," she said. "Apparently your friend Tamsin has had an accident and needs somewhere to recuperate. He wanted to know if you could help?"

"Poor Tamsin," I said. "Of course I'll help. Did he leave a number?"

"Yes, the hospital. It's Doctor Simms. Tamsin is in Ward Nine."

"I'll go and see her at the weekend. Thanks, Mum. It's a good job we have more room."

When Graham came home I told him as much as I knew and he agreed to help get the other bedroom ready for a guest.

"I don't know how badly hurt she is," I said, "but I'll find out on Saturday."

"Did you want me to get time off and take you?"

"Not this time, but you might be needed to move her when she's fit."

I wished I'd asked for more details but it could wait – hospitals were busy places.

Tamsin

My hair was a mess. I ached all over. My face was almost untouched this time but I felt so weak I could hardly stand. I'd tried to get to the toilet but it was too much of an effort. If I was to leave this hospital it would have to be in a wheelchair.

"You can't go for a few days yet," said the nurse, "but you have a visitor."

It was Meg. She looked plumper and more confident than when I had last seen her. Life had obviously been kind to her.

I felt a stab of jealousy. Why was I the one who always got into scrapes?

"Hi, Tamsin," she said. "I've brought some grapes – boring, I know."

"It's great to see you, Meg. I'm so sorry about all this."

"What happened?"

"It was a man. He was jealous. He hit me, but it was a bad time. I was pregnant."

"Oh, Tamsin – did it...?"

100

"I lost it – probably for the best. The fellow was a thug."

"You vanished. Where did you go?"

"I joined a fair. I'll tell you all about it some time – but what about you?"

"I'm lucky. I'm engaged. My fiance and I have a flat and it has two bedrooms. Looks like we're having a lodger for a while."

She smiled her warm, sunny smile.

"You don't mind? He won't mind? What's his name?" She told me about Graham.

"But he's the one I said was boring!" I exclaimed.

"Yes, but he's not. Just wait until you meet him. When will they let you out?"

"When I can walk, I guess. I haven't got much money, Meg. Could you bring a few things for me?"

"Where's your stuff?"

"In a caravan – if Vince hasn't thrown it out. They were going to Sutton next. They'll be there for a week – ask for Mike."

"We will. That's not far from us. Make a list and I'll come back next weekend."

"I'll try."

"Would you like some magazines?"

"Yes please – something that doesn't need much thought."

"OK. I'll go and find some. You rest."

I didn't need much encouragement. I was dosed with painkillers. All I wanted to do was sleep.

Graham

It was curious, having someone else in the flat.

I suppose Meg would have been like this if we'd had a child. Tamsin seemed very childlike – vulnerable and dependent.

Meg said she'd had a torrid time and I tried to be sympathetic but she still felt like an intruder.

At first she stayed in bed in 'her' room but, as she grew stronger, she joined us for meals and most evenings.

She was very different from Meg, with a wicked sense of humour and plenty of stories of her time with the show people.

Meg began to go into her room to plan lessons and I began to feel left out.

"She needs to get her confidence back," said Meg, when I complained. "Once she has a purpose in life we can let her go."

"Will she ever teach again?"

"Probably not – but she could help adults who have had bad experiences. There's something called 'Art Therapy' and I'm trying to get her to consider that."

"Perhaps you could get her to consider a place of her own, too."

"Oh, Graham – you know she hasn't got any money."

I did indeed. Meg and I had driven over to the fairground and met Mike. He took us to the van she had been sharing with Vince and unlocked it.

"Get the stuff you can find while he's not here," he said. "I don't think he'd be very helpful. He's been gone for days."

We couldn't find much that seemed likely to belong

to Tamsin, only a few clothes, but while we were there a young woman came over.

"Are you Tammy's friends?" she asked.

"Yes."

"I'm Sue. How is she?"

"She lost the baby," said Meg, "But she's getting over it."

"Thank goodness. I've got a few of her things. When you've finished here I'm in the pink van."

Sue had, indeed, got some of Tamsin's art work and a handbag full of papers and a small purse containing a few pounds.

"Mike says she's due another fifty," she said. "Sorry it isn't more. She was a wonderful artist."

"She still is," snapped Meg. "She's not dead."

"I'm sorry. I didn't mean to upset you. I guess she'll not be back."

"Not if what she told us about Vince is true."

"Oh, it will be. You'd better leave before he finds you are here."

Everyone seemed terrified of this Vince and if they expected him back I wanted to stay, as I was curious to see him, but Meg pulled me away.

"Let sleeping dogs lie," she said as Mike came over to say goodbye.

"I'm glad she's got friends like you," he said. "Tell her we miss her."

"We will," I replied, seeing Meg was still angry.

Maybe I'd been thinking of myself too much and should make more of an effort to understand her friend.

Tamsin

It was a nice flat, although they'd put me in the front bedroom and the traffic started about 6am.

It was a big room, with a single bed and an enormous desk – perfect for my drawings.

We set up a litle work corner and Meg joined me to plan her lessons.

I'd forgotten how domesticated she was. She'd made thick, lined curtains for my room to try to stifle the noise from outside but I had to sleep with the window open so it rather ruined the effect.

Graham wasn't quite how I had imagined him. He was still quiet and rather unimpressive but, like an iceberg, I felt there was more to him, hidden away.

When they'd come back from the fair they'd asked if I wanted to press charges against Vince, but I hadn't wanted a baby and he'd probably done me a favour, so I said no.

Seeing them together I realised how perfect their union was. They gave each other time – each listening to what the other said. It was like watching a balancing act, or two rowers propelling a canoe.

I drew a cartoon. I couldn't help it. Meg and Graham sitting in a pea green boat, like the owl and the pussycat.

Meg laughed when she saw it. "Tamsin, that's brilliant. I must show Graham."

Graham stared at it and then at me. "You're very perceptive," he said. "You should be drawing for a magazine."

"Oh, I'd not get enough ideas," I replied.

"Try it. Try drawing politicians and people in the

news. You're talented, Tamsin."

I felt as if I had grown two inches while he looked at me. His eyes behind his glasses were bright blue. I don't think I'd ever looked straight into his face before.

He smiled, and I felt myself blush.

Meg was studying the drawing.

"Thanks, Graham," I muttered. "You keep it."

"We will," chimed Meg."We'll get it framed," and she gave a happy giggle.

Most weekends Meg spent Saturday at the shoe shop with her parents.

Graham was usually out nearly all day. I think he was using the library when he wasn't working.

The weather was getting warmer and I felt too lazy to go out. I decided to wash my hair.

I had bleached it when I was pregnant but the roots were showing through. I couldn't afford to go to a hairdresser but I could, at least, keep it clean.

I didn't bother getting dressed and I was towelling my hair, sitting on the edge of the bed, when Graham stopped in the doorway.

"Hallo, you," I said.

"Tamsin. Sorry if I disturbed you."

"You didn't. It's nice not to be left alone."

"How are you feeling now?" He stepped into the room.

"Fabulous." I shook my damp hair at him. "No, really, I do feel better – thanks to you both."

I couldn't help myself. I got up and put my arms round his neck and kissed him.

It wasn't meant to be anything other than a friendly

kiss but his arm went round my waist and he pulled me towards him, returning my kiss and continuing to cover my face with more.

"Graham!" I tried to pull away but he was propelling me back towards the bed.

Then he suddenly stopped.

I fell backwards and lay there, waiting to see what he would do next.

Without a word, he turned and left the room, slamming the door behind him.

Graham

It was like living happily with a ladybird and then, suddenly, finding a butterfly in the house.

Tamsin was so different from Meg.

I loved Meg, of course I did, but she'd been my first steady girl friend. I'd never met anyone quite like Tamsin. She had a vibrant, free thinking aura about her – as if she was ready for anything, accepting what life threw at her and absorbing it.

She was also full of ideas and ready to see the fun in life.

Her caricatures were astounding. She had drawn me as the owl and Meg as the pussycat. There was some truth in that – but when she was around I didn't feel owlish – I felt rebellious, like an outlaw, as if I was tired of playing by the rules.

My whole life was based on imposing rules, seeing that people didn't cheat – but there is a part of everyone that would let them act differently, if they could get away with it.

Then, one morning, I saw Tamsin sitting on her bed, towelling her highlighted hair, wearing only a long Tshirt. Her legs were bare and I could see her shoulder bones in her slender back.

She lifted her head and grinned at me. "Hallo, you." she said.

Her small breasts showed through the thin cotton. I began to feel uncomfortable.

"I'm sorry I disturbed you," I said.

"You didn't. It's nice not to be left alone."

The word 'alone' seemed to hang in the air and I thought how brave she had been about losing her baby.

"How are you feeling ,now?"

"Fabulous."

I didn't hear the rest of her answer. I stood, mesmerised, as she got up and put her arms round me. The air was electric and I felt her wet hair on my face.

She was standing on tip toe and kissing me and before I had time to think my body was responding.

She was warm and lithe and impossibly attractive. She was hardly dressed. It would have been so easy to throw her onto the bed and make love to her. How I wanted to do just that!

"Graham!" she shouted and I realised what was about to happen. If I had continued my whole life would have been ruined. Meg would never have forgiven me.

I felt weak. I pulled away and left the room, my frustration turning to anger as I slammed the door.

Why had this woman come into our lives – and how was I going to continue living with her?

* * *

That night, feeling Meg's ample curves and the heat from her body I found myself comparing the two women again and wondering what it would be like to have sex with Tamsin.

"You're miles away, darling," said Meg. "Anything bothering you?"

"Not really," I lied. "I'm just daydreaming."

"Chopping down trees and finding beetles, I'll be bound," she laughed, softly.

Not quite, I thought, and tried to block the image of Tamsin from my thoughts, but the wretched girl had used Meg's apple shampoo and the scent of her had been the same.

I gave in to Meg's caresses then and reached onto the bedside table for my protection. Once again, I was playing by the rules.

Tamsin

I had a pile of magazines and newspapers and was studying them to discover a 'house style'.

Graham was right. I could probably earn my living as a cartoonist if I could think of witty enough subjects. It wasn't just the drawing that mattered, it was the joke, the punchline.

I had begun to notice more about him, too – how slender his fingers were; how, although his face was tanned glimpses of his body revealed much paler flesh. He was obviously unused to baring his body in the sunshine like the men at the showground had done.

He did, however, sport shorts on warm Sundays and his leg muscles were firm and strong.

The two of them slung backpacks over their shoulders and trudged off to join their group wandering round the countryside most weekends.

I hated Sundays. Walking was not for me and I missed the buzz of a riotous Saturday night. I used to be able to avoid Sunday mornings altogether and woke up just in time to have a bath and an indulgent tea followed by a lazy evening in front of the box.

Without such a weekend I felt caged and irritable. I decided to take the train into town and visit a street market – anywhere where there was colour, people and noise.

It was no use. I felt more lonely in a crowd than I had in the flat.

I was drawn towards a stall with hanging chimes and incense sticks. A young woman, about my age, was putting strange jewellery on display, with semi-precious stones and celtic rings.

The chimes clinked in the breeze, the metallic bells contrasting with the subtle 'clop' of the wooden shapes.

"You'd like one?" she asked, giving the nearest one a tap and making it ring out.

"I don't have anywhere to put it," I said. "Although I do like the sound of the wood."

"It doesn't have to be outside. You can hang them anywhere there's a draught," she coaxed.

"How much?"

She told me. I had enough money but was it something I really wanted?

"They bring good luck," she purred and I gave in. Luck was something I could do with – but it made me think. How much longer could I go on staying with

Graham and Meg? I needed a place of my own- and to get that I needed a job.

I would start the next day, sending out examples of my cartoons to papers and magazines. It hadn't been a wasted day. Now I was determined to start afresh and plan my future.

Margaret

When I came home from work on Wednesday night they were laughing again! Every time I saw them together I envied Tamsin the way she managed to make Graham forget himself.

This time it was over some business cards.

"Look what we've designed,Meg!" called Tamsin. "Graham is so clever."

The cards had a green background with a little cartoon person – looking like an elf, and the words "TAMSIN DEED – freelance artist" and our telephone number.

"Tams – indeed, see?" said Tamsin triumphantly. "It looks better than Greene."

"But that's not your name," I said." Why change it?"

"It's just a pun," said Graham. "I enjoy word games."

"I just feel like being someone new and Graham understands. He's trying out jokes for me, too," boasted Tamsin. "He's a treasure."

"I know," I said. " and I suppose the treasure would like some tea?"

Graham looked guilty then. "I forgot to get the potatoes," he said.

"Never mind. Lets get fish and chips." I was trying to join in the mood. I didn't feel like cooking, anyway.

"Why not? Tamsin's got her first commission," said Graham. "Tell her, Tams."

Tams? That was new.

"Just a Parish Magazine," she said. "It's a start. I just need to get known."

"Great, I'll not be long. I must get changed out of these clothes."

I had to get away or they would sense the jealousy in my voice. Graham and Tamsin? Never. She just wasn't his type.

I looked at myself in the mirror as I got changed. Was happiness making me fat? Had I been too content with my life? Had I stopped trying to be attractive?

I was going to have to try harder for the wedding. I would look for an exercise class. I would never be as slim as Tamsin but I could get fitter.

My thoughts turned to my friend. She'd been a great help, designing the invitations, helping me to choose a dress that flattered me and a bright rose pink silk outfit for her, my only bridesmaid.

She was looking so much happier now she had work to do – and she was beginning to go out at weekends so we had Saturday evenings to ourselves.

She didn't always come home alone but there was never anyone in her room in the mornings. I was glad. She needed company, even if it wasn't the kind we would feel comfortable with.

It was my mother who voiced her concerns. "Do you think you should start married life with a lodger?" she asked, one Saturday.

I was packing shoes into boxes and wondering if I could get away with silver sandals on 'the day.'

"She's been with us for weeks," I said. "I can't throw her out now."

"Could she afford to live on her own?"

"I don't know. She's on some kind of benefit and gets paid for her cartoons. Graham gave her the money for the invitations, but it's not a regular wage."

"Is she ill?"

"Not that I know of – although losing a baby must be pretty devastating."

"Well, I would encourage her to be more independent – give her until September."

"I can't do that, mum. She's my best friend."

"I hope so."

She'd worried me so much. I decided to go back after lunch. Graham often worked Saturdays so I could talk to Tamsin on her own and see what her long-term plans were.

We had been so caight up with the wedding that I hadn't thought it might not be good for her.

Tamsin wasn't at the flat so I walked to the leisure centre and booked an aerobics class. Then I went shopping for leggings and a pair of trainers. The classes were on Monday evenings so I shouldn't be too tired. They were both at home by the time I got back.

When I told her Tamsin was enthusiastic. "Let me know what it's like and maybe I'll join you," she said. It wasn't quite what I had intended but I nodded assent.

Graham was less supportive. "Don't you get enough exercise on Sundays?" he said. "I'd rather you were at home."

"Just because you don't go out in the week there's

no reason I have to stay in." I said.

He looked sheepish, then. He did sometimes go out to see his family but, apart from the library, we seemed to go everywhere else together.

"I'm enjoying my time with you while I can," he muttered. "I may have to spend time away."

I retreated to the kitchen. I didn't want an argument. He could have said I didn't need to exercise, but he hadn't.

Graham

Monday night Meg left for her exercise class. I wished I had somewhere to go – but I'd never been one for pub life. Beside, Tamsin was restless. She'd been looking at a letter from the local vicar for ages.

"What's he say?" I asked,

"He's given me a list of quotes from the Bible. Six month's worth. He says can I do a drawing for each one. Listen..

'God loveth the cheerful giver.'

'I am the Good Shepherd. The good shepherd layeth down his life for the sheep.'

The first one's easy but what do I do for the second – not someone dying!"

"No – I'd just put the sheep in a cosy shed and leave the shepherd out in the cold."

"Great-that should do it – we make a good team, Graham."

She looked so pleased and happy I had to grab hold of her, but it was a mistake. As soon as she got close I could feel the energy in her. I felt stimulated, fascinated and unable to move out of her orbit.

We kissed – and then, as if we had known all along where it would lead went, hand in hand, to her bedroom.

I felt as if I was in the hands of an expert. She teased me and rode me, accepting my tentative gestures with whispered encouragement and kisses.

I couldn't think, I could only feel and afterwards I cuddled into her, greedy for more, but strangely exhausted.

I shouldn't have slept – but I did.

Margaret

People were milling round in the foyer of the leisure centre when I arrived.

"What's happened?" I asked.

"Christine – the woman who takes the exercise class. She isn't coming. We don't know if there is anyone else who could do it."

"Is she ill?"

"I don't think so. Someone said she was being questioned about her link with the Campaign for Nuclear Disarmament."

"CND? Surely they're peaceful?"

"Don't ask me. I'm not into politics."

I looked round for someone in authority but there was a huddle of people in the corner and soon one of them detached themselves from the group.

"We've decided to cancel tonight," she said. "If one of us takes it we aren't insured. We're going to the café for a drink if anyone wants to join us."

It was my chance to meet some of them so I followed along, looking out for anyone who seemed on their own.

One woman looked as if she needed to lose weight so I sat next to her with my coffee.

"Is this your first time?" I asked.

"No. I've been coming since Christmas," she said. "Are you new?"

"Yes. I'm trying to get fit for my wedding."

"Really? Oh, there's my friend Sonia. See you next week," and she took her drink and left me alone.

Still, I hadn't come to find friends. I'd come to feel slimmer, more attractive, more deserving of Graham's love.

I made my way home, leaving my scooter under the steps as usual.

Letting myself in, I glanced into the kitchen and lounge, both empty, and continued down the corridor to the bedrooms. Both doors were closed so I went into our room and took off my helmet and jacket.

Where was everybody? Neither Tamsin nor Graham had said they were going out.

I crossed the corridor to Tamsin's room and pushed the door open a crack. It was gloomy, but not too dark to see the two figures in the bed.

They were covered with a white sheet. Graham was spooned round Tamsin and both of them appeared to be asleep.

Something in my chest felt hard – as if I had swallowed a stone.

I didn't scream or faint. I felt sick but I silently pulled the door to, and went to the kitchen.

There I took the largest saucepan I could find and filled it with cold water. I had to hold it with two hands because I was shaking so much. I wanted to get back to them before they woke up.

Pushing the door open with my knee, I approached the bed.

I think I saw Graham's eyes flicker and he began to lift his head but I swung the saucepan and flung the contents over them with all the force I could muster.

Graham gasped and Tamsin screamed.

I felt a surge of elation. I wished I had more. I wanted to follow it up with smashing something into their faces.

They were both naked and, while Graham lay shivering under the soaked sheet, Tamsin leapt from her side of the bed, looking round for something to cover her.

"Out!" I shouted. "I want you out – both of you. Be gone by the morning. I don't want to see either of you ever again."

I could see Graham was struggling to find words but all that I heard was, "Meg. I'm so sorry."

I didn't want to hear any more. I retrieved my helmet and jacket and went down to my scooter.

I rode rather unsteadily to my parent's shop and let myself in.

They were still up – and there was still a single bed in my childhood bedroom.

"Things have changed," I told them. "I don't think there'll be a wedding," and I finally burst into tears.

Tamsin

The bitch! To come in and deluge me with cold water. That was an underhand trick.

I could have understood it if she had screamed at us – or even started crying – but to treat us like a couple

116

of dogs on heat – when we were asleep! I could have had a heart attack.

OK – so I seduced her fiancé – but they weren't married -and he enjoyed it. I could have taught him some moves he could have used on her. I wasn't jealous. I was adding to their experiences.

I did wonder if Meg would let me stay once she'd calmed down but when I asked Graham he seemed utterly bemused and unable to make a decision.

"You'll have to go somewhere else for a while," I said. "Can you go home?"

"Yes," he mumbled. "Yes, I will. Do you think she'll ever forgive me?"

"I hope so. I expect she'll blame me. I'll have to find a B and B – but I've got so much here - I can't leave, just like that."

So he went – and I stayed to face the music.

Margaret

I rang in sick. I didn't want to let the children down but I couldn't just go to work as if nothing had happened.

I needed to get back to my own home and try to cope with what I had seen.

I had slept, fitfully – after I had told my parents the bare bones of what had gone on. My father was angry but mother told him to leave everything to me.

I was grateful for that. She trusted me to be strong and I was determined. I could not marry a man who could so easily be unfaithful. I thought I knew him – but, obviously, I didn't.

In a way, I blamed myself – for not seeing how

Tamsin was flirting with him – but that was how she had always been.

I went back to the flat mid morning, wondering what I would find.

I found Tamsin.

"Graham's gone to his parents," she said, "but I don't have anywhere to go. Can I stay until I find somewhere?"

It seemed logical. Besides, I wanted to know how it had happened – what wiles she had used to get him in her bed.

"Don't try to be like me," she warned, when I asked her. "You're different. You are for the long term. I'm just a flash in the pan."

"Flash is right," I said, bitterly. "Oh, Tamsin. How am I going to live without him?"

"You aren't. You'll take him back after a while," she said, heartlessly.

"Never. I could never trust him again."

She shrugged.

I had a miserable, lonely evening. Tamsin went out – Looking for some other poor mug, I thought.

It was hard to believe the two people I had felt so close to had betrayed me like that.

I rummaged through the cupboards for chocolate and a bottle of wine. I wanted to blot out the last 48 hours.

I must have dropped off because I was woken by Tamsin's return.

"I've made a decision," she said, not waiting for me to pay proper attention. I tried to focus on her and listen to what she was saying.

"I'm going back on the road," she declared. "This life as a businesswoman isn't really me. I need to be moving about, meeting new people, seeing new places. That would suit you, wouldn't it?"

She seemed almost belligerent. What was I supposed to say?

"You've got so much stuff," I muttered at last.

"Oh, I'll chuck most of that. You can store the important things, can't you? You've got plenty of room."

"When will you go?"

"At the weekend. Good job it's summer. I need new shoes and then I'll be out of your hair. Don't fret. It's the best way to get your man back."

I couldn't believe how unfeeling she sounded. Did she really think I would take Graham back after what I had seen?

My mouth was dry and my head ached. "I'm off to bed," I said, taking a glass of water and a couple of pain killers from the kitchen cabinet. "I have to go back to school tomorrow."

4

LOSS

Tamsin

I hadn't realised how confined I had been feeling in Meg's flat. It was as if I was their pet eccentric.

I had watched and listened to them finishing each other's sentences and laughing at shared memories and felt more and more like an outsider.

I had to get Graham to notice me. I couldn't stand being ignored. But I was sorry I had hurt Meg. She didn't deserve it.

Anyway, I was doing the right thing now – for all of us. I had a change of clothes, a poncho for rain, a sleeping bag and my drawing pad and pencils. I was ready for the next adventure.

"Have you enough money?" Meg asked as I prepared to leave on Saturday morning. What was she-a saint?

"Yes, thanks -and I've told the editor of the parish magazine I'm going – but I've done all the illustrations for the next six issues."

"How will you manage?"

"I'll hitch. I want to go down to Cornwall and if I find another fair on the way I'll join up with them. I just wish I'd got my bike."

"Was it stolen?"

"Appropriated, I think, and I can guess who by – not Vince. If I track down the thief he'll have to pay."

Jake had mentioned that he needed one and I was fairly sure he'd have taken the opportunity to 'take care' of mine in case I returned.

To tell the truth, I didn't feel like riding just then. I decided to take the train to Chertsey and then see if I could find someone going west. I wanted to breathe country air. I was tired of living in town.

Graham

I didn't want to lie to my parents but I couldn't tell them everything. I just said Meg wanted some time to herself before the wedding.

I'm not sure they were convinced but they didn't question me further. I continued to pay my share of the rent on the flat, but I didn't know what else to do.

When I told my sister she, naturally, sided with Meg.

"If she's any sense she'll send you packing for good," she said, "How could you be so stupid?"

"I don't know. I don't know what came over me. Tamsin was so different – so refreshing."

"You're going to have to work hard to get back in Meg's good books," she said, growing serious. "It will take time – but I think you two were made for each other."

"That's what I thought, too," I said, miserably.

"Don't do anything for a few days. I'll ring her and ask about the wedding. If she wants to cancel that's really drastic."

"I'm not sure I'll be able to face her. It's only two months away."

"You'll probably have to cancel it – or postpone. Have you paid the deposit for the reception? Someone will have to inform all the people who have been invited."

"Yes – It's a good job I hadn't booked the honeymoon. I was going to do that this week. We were going to Scotland."

"Leave it until Sunday. If she agrees to your usual walk you'll know you're forgiven, but I don't think it's likely."

I knew Meg better than that. When she'd said she didn't want to see either of us again she'd meant it. I really didn't want to contact her on Sunday, but the wedding loomed over us. I didn't want to cancel it but I had to know how she felt. Was there a chance it could still go ahead?

Margaret

The flat seemed very empty without Graham and Tamsin.

I didn't go to the shop on Saturday. I tried to imagine what my life would be like from now on.

I would have to contact all the people we had invited to the wedding.

I had part paid for my dress – but they hadn't done any alterations so they might keep it.

Graham had booked the Church Hall for the reception. He could contact them. Every time I thought of him I felt hurt and angry.

The best thing I could do was book a holiday for the summer. Where could I go that wouldn't be too hot or expensive?

The Scillies – I would go to a Scilly Island. It was somewhere I had longed to see. I had to get away, and be away for the day when we would have got married.

Then Graham rang, early on Sunday morning.

"Can I see you?" he asked.

"No. Didn't you understand what I said – and you can cancel the wedding. I'll contact the people we invited. I've got the list. You can do everything else."

"We'll need to discuss bills, sometime," he said.

"I know, Mr Right and Proper. I'll write to you next week and make arrangements to take over the rent. I don't want anything from you, ever again."

I slammed the phone down, shaking at the sound of his voice.

But bills were going to be a problem. How could I continue in our lovely maisonette on only one income?

I would need help, and as there was still one person I hadn't told about Tamsin I hoped she might be the answer.

I rang Georgie.

"Meg! It's wonderful to hear from you. Tamsin told me your news. Thanks for the invite."

"I'm afraid that's all off," I said. "There's no wedding. Tamsin saw to that."

"Oh, no. She wasn't up to her old tricks, was she?"

"Yes – with Graham. I've sent them both packing but now I don't know what to do about the flat."

"If I tell you my news, that might help," she said. "I'm giving up teaching at the end of this term. I've been taken on by a model agency in London – but I needed somewhere to stay. I was looking in the Fulham area but you aren't that far out, are you?"

"Georgie! You mean you could come and stay here, with me?"

"It's fate, Meg. As soon as we break up I'll be over."

"It will have to be in July. I've booked three weeks away in August."

"That's OK. I don't start until September. I'm at home for the summer – out of this dreadful flat."

It did seem like fate. Georgie would be a completely different flat mate from Tamsin. I'd not get much of a look in in the bathroom and we'd have to come to some arrangement about visitors – but we could share the cooking and I might be introduced to people in an exciting new line of work.

Of course, the downside was that she was beautiful. It was a good job I'd started my exercise class.

It was hard, fielding all the questions about the cancellation of the wedding.

To most people I just said we had parted by mutual consent.

Mother and father were sympathetic and didn't try to get me to change my mind, although I knew they liked Graham.

Term ended and Georgie was due the next day. I had redecorated the front bedroom in an effort to make it different from when Tamsin was there. It was pale grey with rich cream paintwork. The carpet was practical cream and brown tweed effect. I knew Georgie would have preferred fluffy pure cream but I couldn't afford it. I had bought a new duvet, too, with a gold and grey cover.

The curtains were russet, and didn't quite match the carpet but they did have a cream lining which kept out most of the traffic noise.

I put a vase of freesias on the bedside table and waited.

The bell rang and I went to open the door.

Georgie stood outside, a smart suitcase in each hand – her blonde hair tied back in a bushy ponytail. She was wearing a white jacket, tight blue jeans and white boots. Her eyes were made up as with heavy mascara and turquoise eye shadow and her cheeks were rouged. She looked magnificent.

"Come in," I said and she wafted past me in a cloud of perfume.

"There's another case in the car," she said, "but I must get these boots off. I just can't drive in sandals."

"Is the car locked?" I asked, "or can I get it?"

"It will do, later," she said. "Have you got any lime juice? I'd love a drink."

"Only lemon squash, I'm afraid."

"That will do fine – with lots of ice, please. What a nice flat."

She released her cases and followed me into the kitchen.

"If you'd like to take this into the lounge I'll put your bags in your room," I said.

"Meg, you're a brick. I'll get sorted soon. It was a pretty tricky drive."

She collapsed onto the sofa and I moved her bags from the hall and joined her.

"I've made salad for lunch," I said. "I didn't think you'd want to go out."

"Perfect. Then perhaps we could have a little walk around the area. If you know a nice restaurant I'll treat you to dinner."

I thought quickly – where was somewhere I hadn't been with Graham?

"There's the Station Hotel," I said. "We could try that."

Life was going to be very different with Georgie about.

Tamsin

I thought setting out on a Saturday was a good idea but I'd left it too late. There were cars going in the right direction, of course, but going too fast or obviously too full to stop for me.

Eventually a lorry pulled up a few yards ahead of me and the driver leant over to open the door.

"Where are you headed, love?" he asked.

"Cornwall," I said.

"I'm only going as far as Winchester -but hop in."

He was big, almost bald, with strong tattooed arms. He stank of tobacco smoke but seemed friendly and talked about his family as we drove through the afternoon.

"You'll not get to Cornwall tonight," he said at last

and my heart thumped. Was he going to make a move on me?

"There's a Youth Hostel a mile or two on – would you like dropping off there?"

"That would be great, thanks."

"Rob. Maybe we'll meet up again. Good luck, love."

I had been fortunate. Hitch hiking was always risky. Not everyone was as friendly as Rob.

I had been in youth hostels before, and this was one of the better ones. No privacy – but a hot drink and a bed to sleep on. Trouble was – we weren't near any shops and I was beginning to discover what I was missing.

I needed some basic provisions, bread, cheese and water, and a torch. I craved a big crunchy apple. I would need to find a food shop before I accepted another lift.

In the morning I discovered it was only two miles into the town and I added a map to my mental list.

"You don't have to buy one," said the centre manager. "We have photocopies here for everyone's use."

I didn't think it was allowed but I was grateful. Maybe someone had drawn them – something else I could do, one day.

Next day an elderly couple picked me up in their Allegro. It had plush seats and I sat in the back and fell asleep. I had found a supermarket and stocked up.

They took me to Torquay and I thanked them and got out, my legs stiff and my stomach rumbling.

I sat by the roadside and ate my cheese roll and decided it was time I walked. However, I did not want to use the main road.

I wanted to walk near the coast. It was a bright sunny day and being near the sea made me feel lighter, happier, freer.

I passed a crowded beach and surprised myself at the sense of loss I experienced when I saw the children playing happily in the sand.

Then I climbed a cliff and looked down onto the harbour of Brixham.

All thoughts of travelling to Cornwall left me.

I was on the edge of a caravan site. If I could make myself useful to the owner perhaps, I thought, he would let me stay a while.

I entered a wooden hut that seemed to serve as a reception area.

The young woman behind the counter looked up as I went towards her.

"Can I help you?" she asked.

"I hope so. I'm looking for work."

"What kind of work?"

"Anything. I need somewhere to stay. I've done painting, construction, catering, cleaning and publicity."

"Can you sing and dance?"

"Yes."

"Would you mind dressing in costume?"

"Not at all."

"Well, wait here. I'll see the boss."

The boss turned out to be a large woman with an enormous bust and bright red hair piled on top of her head.

"Cherie says you are an entertainer," she said.

"Among other things," I replied. "I'm looking for work for the whole season – and maybe longer."

"You'll share a van?"

"I've done it before."

"We'll give you a week's trial. Cherie take – what's your name -to van 21."

"T – Trudy," I said, "Trudy Deed." I wasn't going to tell them my name was Greene.

"OK, Trudy. If Lily says it's OK you can bed down with her. See me at four o'clock and you can have some chow. Staff eat before or after the guests."

Now I had to impress this 'Lily' whoever she was. I was hot and tired but I fixed a smile on my face as we entered the caravan.

'Lily' was a waif. She couldn't have been more than fifteen years old and had the thinnest body I had ever seen.

Her dark eyes were set deep in her pale face. Her hair was blonde, a delicate platinum blonde that made her look like someone out of a fairy story.

"Lily, this here's Trudy. She's to share with you," said Cherie, abruptly.

The girl looked at me. She had long dark lashes and I felt I wanted to draw her but instead I said, "Hi, Lily, thanks for letting me share your van."

"S'aint mine," she said, "S'Ma's."

"Ma? Who's Ma?"

"She's the boss's daughter," said Cherie. "Mrs Cracknell to you. I'll see you later."

I was left staring at the nymph-like form of Lily Cracknell.

"That's your bunk," she said, at last. "Maisie used to sleep there."

"What happened to Maisie?"

"She left. She met someone in town."

"A boy?"

"I s'pose. I don't go into town."

"What do you do?"

"I clean up. I wash dishes. I don't dance."

"What kind of dancing do they mean?"

"All sorts, animals, tap, rude. I'm too skinny for that."

"Rude?"

"Yes – dancing when people take their clothes off – on Stag Nights."

"Where does this happen?"

"In the big barn. That's where everything happens."

"Is that where the food is?"

At the word 'food' Lily winced. It occurred to me then – I was in the presence of an anorexic.

If she couldn't hear the word 'food' without reacting, what on earth did she do when faced with the actual substance?

I took a bar of chocolate out of my backpack. "Would you like some?" I asked.

She backed away from me as if I was offering her poison.

"N-No thanks," she said. "I don't eat chocolate."

"Why not, Lily?"

"I don't want to look like my mum," she said and then covered her face with her hands. "I don't want to talk any more," she said, and turned away from me.

I looked round the van "I can use one cupboard, can I?" I asked.

"Yes," she said, pointing to the one nearest my bunk.

There was no clothes rail but shelves and a drawer under my bed. It was enough for my few belongings. I splashed my face and combed my hair and went looking for 'the boss'.

The barn turned out to be the long side of a three sided quadrangle. On the left was a modern looking restaurant, then the barn entertainment centre and, to the right, a supermarket.

The restaurant had formica topped tables and plastic chairs. There was a self-service counter and the smell of cooked cabbage.

I chose fish and chips – hoping that as we were near the sea it might be fairly fresh. The chips were soggy and I didn't think the fish was cod. Still – it was free.

After the meal the boss took me to the barn where I met some of the camp entertainers. They were either young and keen or old and weary.

"We do Bingo, sing songs, children's games and an adult comedy show," said the man who seemed to be in charge. "We have a dance routine that everyone has to learn and a troupe costume that will suit you just fine.

The boss says you're the new Tommy Turtle – that means you'll be in costume all day, get two hours off for a meal and then join us in the evening. We rehearse every morning before breakfast so we'll see you here at 6.30am."

"We all get one day a week off," said a shapely brunette. "I guess yours will be Tuesday. Welcome to the mad house."

So I was expected to start in the morning, was I – and what was the costume for Tommy Turtle?

I didn't get the chance to ask any more questions. The music began and the entertainers disappeared to get changed. The hall was filling up with families and the shutters went up at the bar along one wall.

There was a stage at the end of the room and the space for a dance floor in front of it.

A few children were running round and jumping about to the music, 'The Teddy Bears Picnic.'

Then the tune changed to 'The Grand Old Duke of York' and a tin soldier marched on in front of the curtain.

"Hallo, kiddies!" he called out. "Attention!" and the music stopped. He saluted and most of the children saluted back.

One little girl ignored him and ran through the stationary children as if exploring a maze. Then two entertainers, dressed in white sleeveless tops and very short skirts, came onto the stage, stepped down to the children and began to persuade them to form a circle.

The music started again and the children were herded into the hokey cokey and then a long line for the conga.

Once they had been round the room twice, led by the marching soldier, he dismissed them and the Bingo began.

I'd had enough. If I had to be up at six o'clock I needed to find a toilet and get to bed.

I returned to Lily's van to find her huddled over a magazine.

"What are you reading, Lily?" I asked.

"Just this – about famous people," she said and showed me the page she was on. The story was about an American film star but the page opposite was an advert for beauty products.

I stared at the photograph. It looked very like someone I knew.

"That's Georgie," I said at last.

"No it's not," Lily replied.

"Not the film star – the advert. I know that model. She's a friend of mine. I thought she was still teaching."

"She's beautiful," said Lily, wistfully.

"She always was," I said, " and nuts about makeup and perfume. This is a turn up for the books."

Lily laughed. "You talk funny," she said.

"And how does Tommy Turtle talk?"

She looked serious for a moment. "It isn't easy. It's very hot. I fainted."

"You've been Tommy Turtle?"

"Yes- but it was too heavy for me. You'll see." and she turned back to her magazine.

I undressed and crawled into my sleeping bag. I'd wash in the morning. I was too exhausted to imagine what awaited me the next day.

Margaret

My three weeks in the Scilly Islands had been full of sightseeing. The scenery was beautiful and the hotel was comfortable. I was well fed and entertained and desperately lonely.

Most of the guests were couples or families and the single people were either much older than me or passionate about bird watching or archaeology.

I saw the fantastic gardens on Tresco, but it would have been so much better with someone. Graham would have loved it.

I was glad to get home and start preparing for the new term at school.

Living with Georgie was a revelation.

First, she reorganised my kitchen – buying new equipment, a coffee machine and a blender.

Then she added another cabinet to the bathroom and a new dressing table to her bedroom. The wardrobe already had a full length mirror or I'm certain she would have bought that, too.

She made the evening meal every day, unless she was out – but we had a wall chart in the kitchen that showed all her appointments for the next three months.

I began to realise how Tamsin had found her mixture of overwhelming bounty and officiousness irritating. She had an air of superiority that she didn't seem to realise could alienate people.

I wondered how well that went down with advertisers and photographers.

Most of her work seemed to be in London although she sometimes went abroad for anything up to a week and I had the place to myself.

It was then that I contacted Graham at his parents' house and told him I no longer needed his contribution to the rent.

"We'll have to sign your share over to Georgie," I said. "I'll send you the forms."

"Couldn't we meet up to do it?"

"No. I don't want to see you, ever again."

I should have been married. Instead my life was full with extra responsibility at school. I was to organise the parent-teacher Christmas fair.

I also had the class ready to go up to Senior school. The range of ability was enormous, from children so literate they were reading classics like Jane Eyre and Wuthering Heights to those who could barely write a sentence and still read like seven year olds.

I spent hours every night trying to match the work to the abilities of each set. I wanted so much not to let the slower children feel inferior. I believed that every child should be encouraged to find something they could be good at. It was easy when they excelled at sport or art but harder when I had to reward 'helpfulness' 'neatness' or 'punctuality.'

We had a star chart for our times tables and spellings but I also gave stars for effort and consideration.

If I could show how much I disapproved of bullying at this age I hoped the lesson would last a lifetime.

5

CHANGE

Graham

I had to get on with my life. There was nothing tying me to the London area any longer. I could go anywhere and do anything.

There was a place in the Wye Valley if I wanted, part work placement, part training course. It was exactly what I had longed for – although the money was less than I had been earning I no longer had to pay towards the flat. I could live in a hostel and spend most of my time among the flora and fauna of the woodland.

Being in a natural environment was soothing and the practical activities made me feel fitter and stronger. I was as happy as I could be without Meg.

At first the other trainees laughed at me. I had no strength in my arms and wore spectacles for reading. I suppose I was hardly the 'lumberjack' type.

Yet when it came to learning about plants and animals I found it easy and watching raptors over the valleys I could identify them faster than many of the others.

"You've got long sight," said one of the tutors. "Have you thought of taking up photography?"

I hadn't. I'd always though that was for arty types like Tamsin. I was more of a words and figures man – but I told my parents and they bought me a camera for my birthday.

At the end of the year I had passed all the tests necessary to continue and was half way to becoming a fully fledged forester.

Margaret

Georgie was beginning to worry me. It wasn't that she had no success. She was the face of a new range of beauty products and when she was home she was friendly and generous.

It was just that she seemed to spend more and more time away from the flat.

On one of her rare visits I questioned her. "Georgie, have you got a boyfriend?"

She looked up from the salad she had been preparing. "Yes, I suppose so," she admitted. "Only not so much a boyfriend as an admirer."

"He's older than you?"

"Yes, and he's loaded."

"Do you love him?"

She thought for a minute. "I suppose I do. He's all I ever wanted in a man – but it's a secret."

"Oh, Georgie – he's not married, is he?"

"No – he's divorced, but he's in an important

position. He travels a lot so we get to see each other when we are abroad but when he's in this country we have to be discreet."

"Well, that explains a lot. I don't suppose you'll tell me who he is."

"I can't, Meg. I've told you too much already. It's best you don't know."

"As long as he makes you happy."

"He does. He spoils me. He's bought me a yacht."

"What will you do with that?"

"Sail it, of course – with a crew. I'll just be lazing about on deck with a glass of champagne and a white bikini."

She laughed – but it was a hollow laugh as if she knew there was something missing in her vision.

Tamsin

As summer turned to autumn I expected to be dismissed. Most of the entertainers left and at the end of October there were few bookings. Some of the vans were 'residential' for nine months and were still occupied.

I had been 'Tommy Turtle' for the whole season, completely encased in a plastic and cloth outfit like something from a poor man's disneyland, amusing the children, organising games and then in the evenings, dressing in one of the skimpy costumes designed to make us look sexy for the adults.

Then I was called into the boss's office.

"In the winter we have block bookings," she said. "There's a Country and Western week, a Jazz week, a Sixties week and a Twenties week. Then there's the

Folk week and that's in a fortnight's time. We'd like you to stay on."

"No more Tommy Turtle?"

"No – but you need to dress accordingly each week. See Joyce. She'll kit you out."

I expected the 'folk' look to be a long brown dress with no adornments but I was wrong. I was kitted out like the principal boy in the pantomime Robin Hood.

"Your boss has a thing about legs," I grumbled.

"You'd better watch out," warned Joyce, "She has some strange ideas altogether."

I began to think Lily was right to be disturbed by her mother.

Lily was worrying me. I never saw her eat. She sometimes had a cup of tea with me in the mornings and I found the odd sweet wrapper in the bin but I never saw her in the restaurant and the only food we had in the caravan was bought by me.

One day I found her nibbling a dry biscuit and challenged her about it.

"I don't like fat," she said. "Milk makes me sick and I'm not eating animals."

"If I get a vegeburger will you share it?"

"Perhaps. It has to smell right."

It seems she had been traumatised by a fire when she was younger and even the smell of cooking made her feel ill. She needed therapy but I couldn't do it.

The folk groups began to arrive and were housed in the best vans.

I hadn't done the programme. I could have made a much better job of it than the one they supplied, but I turned up on the first evening ready to parade about in my 'Robin Hood' costume, leather jerkin over an open necked shirt, green tights and high heeled boots.

Our job was to greet the punters, see them seated and take orders for meals and drinks.

I didn't follow the folk scene and didn't recognise the bands until half way through the evening when someone I had seen before stepped onto the stage, holding a guitar.

Behind him were two others, a bass guitarist and a harmonica player.

His hair was longer. He looked tanned. My pulse raced. It was Jake.

He played a couple of familiar tunes and the audience clapped along and applauded enthusiastically.

Then he announced one of his own songs, a wistful lament. The hall grew silent as the quality of his playing became apparent. He made the instrument sing, his rapid fingering almost too intricate to follow and his voice seemed to caress my ears. I didn't want him to stop.

When he did, the reaction was disappointing. People still clapped, but I had the feeling they preferred tunes they knew and could join in with.

I looked at the programme. What did they call themselves? I wondered, 'The Moonlightermen?

'The Downland Rovers?'

There was an interval before the next act and I ran backstage to catch Jake.

"When did you get back from Nottingham?" he asked.

"Don't tease. I just came to say how wonderful I thought you were. I'm sorry I bothered."

"No, really. It's great to see you. I didn't realise you were such a dish, and your hair is better long."

I'd left it loose and it had been growing for quite a while.

"Are you here for the whole week?" I asked.

"Just three days. When do you get time off?"

"Hardly ever."

"Well, I'll come and sit in the audience. You can be our serving wench!"

I did serve them, and they had plenty to drink but I was rushed off my feet and didn't have time to talk. When the evening ended I was too tired to watch where they went.

Lily was washing glasses behind the bar and we finished up and walked home together. She was singing a folk song as we entered the van.

"That's a pretty tune," I said. "Do you like folk music?"

"Yes. This is the best week of the year."

Next morning I woke early and went onto the cliff top to think.

Was this what life was going to be like for me in the future? Would I always be living on campsites and playing Tommy Turtle? Surely there was more to life than that.

I returned to find the van empty. Lily must have gone to the bar to help clean up ready for the next music session.

I could hear a band rehearsing and followed the sound. It wasn't coming from the barn. The Downland Rovers were giving an impromptu outside concert and

Lily was in the front row of the audience.

Suddenly she joined in with the song – her voice delicate and pure, and I saw Jake put out his arm to beckon her to join them.

He stood back, strumming his guitar and let her take his place.

After a hesitant look at him she relaxed and continued, with Jake harmonising behind her.

The small group of people gathered to listen clapped when the song ended and she blushed and came over to join me.

"That was beautiful, Lily," I said. "Jake was very impressed."

"You know him?" she asked.

"Yes. We've met before. Come and talk to him."

The band was dispersing and people were wandering off to get breakfast. Jake came towards us. He ignored me.

"What's your name, love?" he asked Lily.

"Lily. Lily Cracknell."

"Lily cracker, more like," he laughed. "You have a lovely voice. Do you know many folk songs?"

"Some."

"Lily and I share a van, " I butted in.

"Great," he said. "Let's go. We have a proposition for you both."

I knew Lily wouldn't mind missing breakfast but I was hungry. Still – I wasn't going to let her have Jake to herself. We wandered back to the van.

"Tammy," he began as soon as we sat down. "We need a manager. Would you consider the job? You'd need to come with us, of course, and do all the advertising and promotional stuff. I think you'd be perfect. How about it?"

"I don't know people in the business. I'd need to research venues. I haven't got contacts."

"We knew that – but we're hopeless at the business side. We think we could trust you."

"Thanks."

He didn't wait for another answer. He turned to Lily.

"Lily, would you join us, too? You'd add something really special to the group."

"You'd have to change the name," I said. "You sound like a football team."

"There, you're thinking like a manager already."

Lily was silent. Then she lifted her head and looked at Jake. That look said it all.

"I would like to be part of your group," she said, softly, "and if Trudy is coming too, that would be wonderful."

It wasn't me that was wonderful, I thought. She'd fallen for Jake in a big way.

He held out his hand to her and she shook it.

"Are you under contract?" he asked me, "with whatever name you're using?"

"I've not signed anything," I replied.

"Then you can both come with us at the end of the week."

"Hold on. Lily, how old are you?"

"Sixteen."

"Then I bet you can't leave without parental permission."

"Oh dear. I didn't think of that." She seemed to shrink into herself.

143

"Don't fret," said Jake. "We'll sneak you out in the van. Don't tell anyone."

I would leave that up to him. I wasn't going to tell the boss.

He was about five years younger than me and I fancied him rotten but I couldn't compete with 'Fairy Tinkerbell.' could I?

I'd have other chances and now I was about to change my image. I would become Tam Greene– and to celebrate that I would get my hair cut and coloured. I always preferred being a redhead and that would help me to think my way into my new role – manager of Jake's group.

With Lily fronting the band I had the perfect name "Pink and Blue." The opportunity for colourful promotional material was immense.

I told Jake. "You don't do all traditional stuff, do you?" I said. "How about a more modern, slicker name?"

"What did you have in mind?"

"Pink and Blue – it has overtones of girl and boy and jazz."

"It's interesting. I'll ask the others. They didn't like Downland Rovers, either."

Great I thought and I wouldn't stop there. If that worked I would find more people to represent. It was an exciting new challenge – and I was up for it.

Margaret.

It was the end of the summer term and a number of the teachers from school were going out on Friday evening for a meal.

I hadn't felt sociable for months and decided it was time I pulled myself together and joined them.

It was a pub I had never used, in Perivale, and I ordered steak and kidney and pudding. It wasn't a dish Georgie ever cooked.

"What are you drinking, Margaret?" asked Roy, the deputy head.

"Cider, please," I replied. I was thirsty.

As we were finishing our desserts the landlord announced that a folk group would be performing in ten minutes.

"Charge your glasses, now, please," he called out.

"I didn't expect entertainment," I said as Roy brought my drink.

"It's Friday night. They always put something on – but we don't have to stay if it's rubbish."

"Ladies and Gentlemen – a big hand for 'Pink and Blue' with their lovely lead singer -Lily."

A slim blonde in tight jeans and a white blouse fronted the band, a guitarist, a harmonica player and a double bass.

Her first song was 'Strawberry Fair' and her voice had a lilting, bell-like quality.

When she continued with 'Cockles and Mussels' I looked at the audience.

Those who had been chatting while they ate ceased and everyone was watching the stage.

Then a thin red-headed figure in a lime green trouser suit came from the side of the stage and took her place at a table in the corner on which there were a selection of raffle prizes.

Even from the back, the person was familiar. It

was Tamsin – a very different Tamsin. Instead of the wild looking hippy she looked composed, calmer and connected, somehow, to the band.

Was she a groupie, or married to one of them?

I studied the men in turn. The bass player was tall, heavily built, with a mournful face. The harmonica player was young, bird-like, full of energy. I could imaging him with Tamsin.

The guitarist, who was now introducing a self-penned song which he sang as a duet with Lily, had a kind of timeless grace, his long hair tied back in a pony tail. He was the one I would have chosen, but they all looked younger than my friend.

The song finished, the audience applauded and I stood up and made my way forward.

Just as I reached her table Tamsin turned and I saw the eager greeting die on her lips as her face changed from delight to concern.

She had no reason to be alarmed. My first instinct was to reach out and hug her. She had been my friend for so long – and whatever had happened between her and Graham had been his fault as much as hers, and mine, in a way, for not anticipating it, knowing what she was like.

She relaxed into my arms.

"Oh, Meg, it's wonderful to see you again," she said.

"You're looking great, Tamsin," I replied. "Are you with the group?"

"I'm not Tamsin any more. I'm Tam. I'm their manager. Don't you think they're something special?"

The guitarist was playing a solo – a haunting, intimate melody and the crowd in the room were almost silent.

I sat down next to Tamsin and watched them finish the set with a roaring sea shanty that got everyone joining in.

The barman announced that raffle tickets would be on sale during the interval and the buzz of conversation resumed.

"I'm with the rest of the staff from my school," I said. "I should get back."

"Stay. I'll introduce you to the band. We're planning to release a record."

I gave my colleagues a wave and waited for the group to join us. The harmonica player brought a tray of drinks - three beers and what looked like lemon and lime for Lily.

She had bright blue eyes and watched the guitarist's every move.

"This is Jake," announced Tamsin. "Simon, Dale,this is Meg, a dear friend."

"Hi Meg" said Jake, " Meet Lily."

The girl looked shy but held out her hand and I took it. It was cool and bony. She looked like she could do with a good meal.

"Your singing's lovely," I said and she smiled. "Thanks."

We were interrupted by a young woman selling raffle tickets and when people began to come up to talk to the band I thought it best to move.

"See you later," I said to Tamsin and returned to my table.

"You know the band, then?" said Roy.

"Only the manager. She used to teach and she stayed with me for a while."

"She looks fit."

She does, I thought – whatever persona she adopted she always looked interesting.

Suddenly I didn't want to be there any more. This woman had stolen from me the one thing that made my life complete -the man I had expected to spend the rest of my life with, and yet, to her it was just another conquest. She hadn't loved him, she'd just used him and not even stopped to consider how much she was hurting me.

Maybe, to her, it was just a meaningless incident. She hadn't realised I would react as I did. To her it wasn't enough to destroy a relationship. To me it had been more than I could bear.

She hadn't asked me if Graham had come back. She didn't know that the hole they had worn in my heart had never healed.

There was wine on the table and I poured a glass, taking a large mouthful, and then another.

I wanted to blot out the memory of the two of them together. I was confused, disturbed and had to get out, away from the noise and the chatter and the music.

I pushed through the crowd to the door and almost tripped on the steps as the night air hit me.

Someone was standing in the shadows. It was Dale, the bass player.

"Going already?" he said.

"No – just getting some air," I muttered, knowing I did not mean to return.

"Tell Tamsin, or Tam, I'm still at the flat," I said, "and there's someone else there she might like to meet again."

I'd forgotten all about Georgie.

"Here's the phone number." I reached into my bag and tore a page out of my notebook.

Standing under the window I squinted in the dim light as I wrote down our number.

Handing it to him, I staggered inside to tell the others I was leaving.

It wasn't more than a mile. The walk would do me good.

By the time I reached the flat the affection I had felt for Tamsin and the anguish she had caused had balanced each other out and I was just exhausted.

Georgie was home, and still up.

I made a coffee and flopped into a chair.

Georgie sat opposite me at the table.

"Did you have a good night?" she asked.

I burst into tears.

"Meg? What's the matter? What happened?"

"Tamsin was there. She's with a band. She looks great."

"Tamsin? She's back?"

"Not really. She's travelling about."

"Did she say anything about Graham?"

Hearing his name sobered me up and I took a sip of my coffee before I answered.

"No. I didn't talk to her much. I just left. I gave the band my number. She'll probably be in touch."

"You poor thing – and here was I, waiting to give you my news."

"Go on, then."

"It doesn't seem the right time."

"Oh, Georgie, if it stops me moping about the past

it will be OK. Is it good news?"

"Yes – I think so. I've had a proposal. I'm getting married next spring."

"Your man friend?"

"Yes. It will be in a hotel in Gloucestershire. You will come, won't you?"

"Of course. I'm really happy for you."

"I'd like Tamsin to be there, too – if it wouldn't upset you."

"No – I'm over that now." I'd stopped crying. "It was fate. I've forgiven her. I just needed to sort things out in my own head."

"And you have?"

"I think so."

I thought I was being honest – but a tiny part of me still wondered what had happened to Graham.

Tamsin

I slept badly that night and woke early

We weren't often up for breakfast but I ate alone and called the number Dale had given me.

What was the mystery Meg had hinted at? Who could be living with her?

I soon found out. The voice that answered the phone wasn't Meg's. It was Georgie.

I'd have recognised those deep, cultured tones any-where.

"Georgie?" I said. "Are you staying with Meg?"

"Yes, Tamsin. I live here now – but not for much longer. Can you come over?"

"The band have a booking in Essex tonight but I

could pop in for an hour or two. Give me directions."

"I'll do better than that. I'll come and get you. Half an hour?"

I told her where we were staying and let Dale know what was happening.

There was giggling coming from Jake's room as I went past. Lily must have been in there. I'd lost out to a younger, prettier woman.

I no longer cared. I was on the lookout for more people to manage, and an office. I probably couldn't afford to set up in London but I fancied Brighton.

I really needed a break from the band so that I could scout around.

I had already decided that when they went up north I would stay south and visit some holiday camps in search of more talent.

I knew how to drive but I hadn't been able to afford a car of my own. I needed money, a sizeable loan, to get me to the next stage.

I was about to check out the east coast camps and then work my way down through Kent to Sussex but I needed wheels. To become successful I needed to look successful.

A sleeping partner would be perfect. It would even look more professional on business cards.

Who did I know who had money, influence and business sense? I'd been making contacts and Georgie would be a great help there. She mixed with 'arty' types as well as establishment figures from her family background.

Could the answer be waiting outside in the silver sports car? Gina, the model or Georgina the ex-teacher?

* * *

"You don't have a chauffeur, then?" I teased as Georgie drove back to the flat.

"Not yet," she said, smiling. "I like my independence – but that may be about to change."

"How? Tell me."

"When we get indoors. So much has happened since we were together. You've changed, too. You look happier."

"I'm getting there. I still get fidgety. I don't like routine. I'm always searching for new ideas, new people, new places to go."

"I can't imagine you in the world of contracts and bookings – but you always were good at the artistic side."

"Yes, I design all the promotional material for the band."

Georgie slowed up outside my old home. "I'll park in the side street," she said, "I don't suppose it's changed much since you were here."

The flat felt different without Graham – more feminine. There was a hint of perfume about the place and the kitchen was full of gadgets. Georgie had made her mark.

"Tea or wine?" she asked.

"I'd prefer coffee."

"Right – coffee it is," she said and filled the filter machine. No instant coffee for our Georgie!

She brought a tray through to the lounge and then looked at me with a proud smile on her face.

"Now for my news," she said. "I'm getting married."

"That's great," I replied. "What's his name and what's he like?"

"I'll show you a picture. He's older than me but we've been together for months. He's the kindest, most generous man I have ever met. The wedding's in Gloucester. I hope you can come."

She went into the bedroom and brought out a framed photograph.

She was on a beach, loking glamorous in a white bikini with a flimsy skirt half covering her legs.

Beside her stood a man who could only be called mature.

He had white hair and a white moustache. He was wearing grey trousers and a navy blazer and had an erect stance that looked almost military.

"He looks very special" I said.

"He is. He has businesses all over the world. His name is Gregory. We're the two 'G's."

"That's wonderful, Georgie. No wonder you seem so content."

"Yes – but I don't want to be a trophy wife. I'd like to contribute something useful to society."

It was my cue. I couldn't believe she had given me such a perfect opening.

"I have an idea," I began. "How would you like to be a part of what I do? I'm looking for a partner – well, finance, really. I need to expand. Would you be interested?"

"In managing groups?"

"Well, in having your name on everything. We'd have to have a contract, work out the details, but if I can find more acts I might start to make a profit."

"How much would you need?"

"First, I need a vehicle. Then I'd need an office. Then

I'd need enough money to get us started. I've been working on a business plan but I didn't have a name: Greene and Mason, or Mason and Greene?"

"Well, it would be a way to keep my maiden name alive. You'll probably need at least twenty thousand pounds. It would be my money, you understand, not Gregory's. This would be our baby – and I'd want to be involved in what was going on."

"You'd come to the gigs?"

"Too right, I would. I'd help get your acts on talent shows on TV. I'd want to know if you discovered someone special.

"Gregory might not want me to continue modelling but this could be something he approves of. It's a fabulous idea, Tamsin. I'm so glad we met up again."

I told her, then, about my plans to travel round the holiday camps.

"You find a car you want and I'll buy it," said Georgie. "It will be a gesture of faith in you. Does it matter where your office is? I might know somewhere, down by the coast. It would do for a start, although you'd probably do best in London."

I could hardly believe the enthusiasm in her voice. "Where would that be?" I asked.

"Shoreham Beach. There's an artistic community down there that make films."

"Georgie, you're brilliant. It must be fate."

"Don't get too excited. You've a lot of work to do. Sort out a proper contract – put all the costs on paper with your business plan and let me have it as soon as possible. This will surprise Gregory."

"He won't be annoyed?"

"Not if it looks efficient. He's a pussycat. Just wait 'till you meet him."

"You won't keep this a secret?"

"No – of course not. He approves of initiative and as this is something I can do at a distance, part time, and still be at home for him it should suit us perfectly."

"Where's home?"

"Usually Warwickshire, but he's always moving about. He owns hotels in Brighton, Bath, Malta and Florida and has offices in London. I've been all over the world with him but I've never found out where his roots are."

"I hope you don't get stuck out in the wilds."

"We might get a second chauffeur, although I like driving. It's a different life, Tamsin. It's more than I ever dreamed of."

She looked so happy I dared to think that the fairytale might come true for her at last and that at least one of us had found her prince, although he wasn't quite as described in story books.

The car I chose was a mini – but, on Georgie's insistence, I had it re-sprayed green.

We had chosen a soft apple green for the background to all our promotional material with 'Greene and Mason',entertainment promotion, in bold black type.

The 'office' she had found for me was a wooden chalet bungalow. It was minutes from the beach and I loved it.

I felt reluctant to take money for clothes from the account we set up but I wanted to look the part.

Brighton had the kind of shops where I could find

items that fitted my new image – smart but sassy – businesslike but different, original, lots of orange, lemon and lime, with shoulder pads and gold buttons. I favoured trouser suits and high heeled boots but chose long cotton skirts and sandals for the hotter weather.

My hair was now in a fashionable 'pixie' cut. I was trying to make an impression and I began by travelling up to Essex.

All the acts there were mediocre but when I moved on to Southend I found a colourful rock group with promise and signed them up.

In Margate I found a speciality act – a group that did music and comedy, but Dover was a washout.

Then, in Hastings, I struck gold.

The camp was full of the usual contests – knobbly knees, lovely legs etc. and one was an Elvis impersonator. The boy that won was exceptionally good and undiscovered.

He was under eighteen and heading for University but I persuaded him he would supplement his income if he joined me.

He was flattered and, after checking with his parents, promised to come on board. Greene and Mason were in business.

Margaret

With Georgie full of wedding plans I had, once again, to decide what to do about the flat when she left.

I was earning enough to keep it on, at least in the short term, but it was full of memories and I felt like a change.

I had thought I would be the first of us to get married

156

and I knew I would feel lonely once she had moved on.

Tamsin was going to live at the coast and Georgie would be over in the West Country.

I needed to find myself a new challenge, new friends, new opportunities.

I began to look in the Educational supplements for vacancies.

I didn't want to go too far from my parents and the shop but I wanted to be surrounded by trees and fields and hear birds instead of traffic.

A village school in the Chilterns was advertising for a teacher. It meant having two year groups in one class because it was only a small school, but there was accommodation.

Half the building was set aside for the head but the present incumbent was married, with a family, and so didn't occupy it. It meant the salary was less than I was getting but, all in all, a very tempting prospect.

I hadn't gone back to the walking group – not without Graham – and I thought that if I moved to the country I would get a dog.

Meanwhile, I had Georgie's wedding to prepare for.

It would be a big, lavish, do - with her parents and her fiancé both trying to show how well off they were.

The press would be there. After all, how often does a millionaire businessman marry one of the most famous models in the country?

It was an odd match. She was at least thirty years younger than him – but the way she spoke she seemed to be in love.

She said she was getting married in pale pink so I wasn't to wear white or red.

I went shopping for a blue two piece but when I got into the store I found an elegant grey dress and jacket that looked nothing on the hanger but fitted beautifully.

I'd lost a bit of weight and, with a possible interview in mind, I decided it would be perfect.

I could dress it up for the wedding with silver jewellery and wear it with black accessories when I went for my next job.

I was booked into the hotel where the reception was to be held.

It wasn't to be a church wedding, as Gregory had been married before.

I would go down early the previous day and stay until the Sunday. It would be good to have the three of us together – maybe for the last time.

Graham

My sister rang with the news.

"There's a letter for you," she said. "It looks like an invitation. Shall I open it?"

"As long as it isn't from the tax man – yes. I wasn't expecting anything. Most people know where I am."

I heard her tearing the envelope and she squealed, "It's a wedding invitation!"

I didn't know a heart could sink so abruptly. Not Meg – my Meg!

My sister was speaking. " There's a letter with it. It's from Tamsin. Do you know a Tamsin?"

"Yes" I stuttered. "She's a friend of Meg's. Whose wedding? Tamsin's?"

"No. It says 'Mr and Mrs Charles Mason invite

Mr Graham Harris to the celebation of the wedding of their daughter Georgina to Mr Gregory Lightfoot on Saturday. Hey, it's next month – can you go?"

"Where is it?"

"Gloucester – not far from you. Why have they invited you?"

"I think I can guess. Read out Tamsin's letter."

"She says she and Georgie wanted you to come. She's sorry she caused so much trouble and she hopes you can take this opportunity to get back to how you were before she arrived on the scene. Does she mean Meg?"

"Of course she does. She means she'll be there."

"And you can make up?"

"I don't know about that. Weddings are funny things. People get very emotional. I'd have to get Meg on her own."

"But you'll go, won't you? You do want to get back together with Meg?"

"I'll think about it."

I could feel my heart beating faster. I'd poured all my energy into work. I hadn't thought about dating or even noticed other women.

Perhaps, in the depths of my mind I was hoping to get back with Meg. Now I was a qualified ranger with prospects I prayed I could be forgiven.

Well, now I had my chance, thanks to Tamsin. It would have been her idea to invite me.

"Send me the lot," I said, "The letter and the invitation. It looks like I need to reply to both."

Tamsin

My scheme worked. Georgie agreed that she should invite Graham Harris to the reception and hoped that he and Meg could be reunited.

The actual ceremony was to be a family affair at the Shire Hall but the reception, or 'celebration' as it was called on the invitations, was at the Castle Hotel a few miles out of town.

Georgie said she would sort out the seating plan so that Graham and Meg sat next to each other and I would be there to keep an eye on proceedings.

The rest was up to them.

I didn't wear green. I had plenty of our new business cards with me but I was there to support a friend, not promote a business.

Nevertheless it would be good to see and be seen, especially as it was a circle I didn't usually mix with.

I chose cream. My hair always looked good with cream. With a cream and green paisley scarf and emerald earrings I was sure I would not have the same outfit as the mother of the bride.

If Georgie was in pink the other women would probably choose blue. I would have done, anyway. It would look good in the photographs.

It turned out I was half right.

Gregory's mother was no longer alive and Georgie's mother was in turquoise.

Only close family had been at the registry office and I couldn't see Meg or Graham at the bar while we waited for the happy couple.

Everyone congregated on the steps of the hotel, filling the balcony and waving as the wedding car drew up on the gravel drive.

People were smiling and taking pictures. I searched the crowd for Meg and spotted her, almost hidden behind a pillar.

Georgie and Gregory got out of their car and started up the steps. People had to move out of the way to let them through, the crowd was so dense.

Georgie's long dress had a wide 'boat' collar and long sleeves. There was no train – just a shaped skirt so that it was shorter in the front than the back.

Her long, blonde hair was down and studded with what looked like diamonds. She looked radiant.

Gregory, of course, looked more like her father than her husband, but he scrubbed up well and seemed very proud of her.

He held her elbow as they went into the foyer and were greeted by the manager. There was a short conversation and then it was announced that they would join us in the restaurant in twenty minutes and we filed in to find our places.

Margaret

I'd never been to a wedding that wasn't in a church before.

The press had been encouraged to take pictures in Gloucester so that they would not intrude on the reception.

When the bride and groom arrived there was a big cheer from the assembled guests and then we moved into the restaurant to find our places at the tables.

Georgie had changed into a shimmering golden off the shoulder gown.

The 'diamonds' were gone from her hair which had been swept to one side. She looked like a film star.

Each square table seated eight people and five of the places were already filled when I got there.

As I had come on my own I wasn't surprised to see I had been flanked on one side by a couple and on the other a lone, elderly, woman.

Next to her was another couple and the two seats opposite were empty.

I introduced myself to the woman on my right who turned out to be Georgie's headmistress when she was a schoolgirl.

The two couples were neighbours of her parents.

Then I saw Tamsin heading towards us, with a man just behind her. I wondered if she'd brought a date.

Recognition dawned as the pair sat down. She was with Graham!

Graham and Tamsin were sitting opposite me, smiling as if nothing had happened.

Tamsin looked flushed and distracted as Graham introduced them.

"I'm so happy you're here," he said, holding out his hand across the table.

I nearly choked. I wanted to get up and rush out.

Were they completely insensitive?

I touched his hand with my fingers and nodded at Tamsin – the snake I had thought was my friend.

The starters arrived and the celebrations began.

I vowed to ignore them as much as possible and leave as soon as I could.

Tamsin

It couldn't have been worse.

Instead of seating Graham next to Meg as I had requested he had been placed next to me.

I wasn't near enough to Meg to explain. It looked as if Graham and I were a couple.

I couldn't eat. I was watching Meg and wondering what she was thinking.

I just wanted the meal to be over and hoped that, somehow, Graham could rescue the situation.

He seemed puzzled by the arrangement but ready to take advantage of meeting Meg again.

He was being polite and listening to the couple on his right.

It seems they were farmers and the conversation was about cattle and badgers.

"How do you know Georgie?" asked the man to my left and I explained about college.

I couldn't face the prawn cocktail, nibbled at the chicken and pushed the fancy trifle round the dish. Meg was doing the same.

The whole day had been ruined for both of us.

We clapped at the speeches, cheered when the cake was cut and drank the champagne. At least, I drank the champagne. It seemed that Meg didn't even feel she could do that.

I couldn't bear the tension.

I got up from the table and gestured to her to follow me. The waiters were bringing coffee and slices of cake.

She shook her head to indicate she would not follow me so I went round the table and whispered in her ear. "He's not with me. I invited him so that.." But I couldn't finish.

"YOU invited him," she hissed.

"I mean – I suggested they invite him – so that he could meet up with you again."

But she wasn't listening. She was rigid with anger.

I saw Graham stand up to come over but before he could reach us Meg had pushed back her chair, barged past me and stormed out.

"Graham?" I appealed – hoping he could catch her and explain, but we were too late. Some of the guests were beginning to drift into the ballroom and she was lost in the crowd.

He turned to me. "What can I do, Tamsin?"

"Find her. We can't leave it now," I said. "She must be in a room here. It can't end like this."

Graham

It was wonderful seeing Meg again. She looked elegant and beautiful.

I wished I had been seated next to her but, at least, with her opposite, I could watch her and there would be time after the meal to pick up where we left off.

I was too optimistic. She obviously thought Tamsin and I were together. I would put her right, I thought, as soon as the meal was over.

Eventually Tamsin got up and went round the table to talk to her.

I watched them both, Tamsin trying to explain and Meg getting more and more enraged. I had to intervene. Meg had misunderstood. Tamsin wasn't getting through.

I stood and went to join them but Meg was too quick for me. She almost spat at Tamsin and, without a glance in my direction, strode out of the room.

I couldn't catch up with her. By the time I got to the door she had vanished.

"What can I do?" I asked.

"Find her," Tamsin replied – but I had the dreadful feeling that it was too late and I had lost the chance to redeem myself in the eyes of the only woman I had ever loved.

6

RESOLUTION

Margaret

I packed. There was no way I was going to stay to be humiliated by those two.

I couldn't believe it. To sit there – as brazen as anything! He even smiled at me as if nothing had happened.

He didn't realise his smile made my heart thump and I dare not grip his hand in case it sent an electric shock through my body.

I hadn't got over him. I might never get over him – but I didn't need to see him with someone else, especially Tamsin.

What a disaster the weekend had been and now I would have to leave without saying goodbye to Georgie. I couldn't bear to be among the guests at this event any longer.

It should have been my wedding we had first – not Georgie's.

The more I thought about it the nearer to tears

I became.

The receptionist found me a taxi to take me to the station.

At least, I thought, as I sat on the train, I would soon be out of the flat and in my new house.

My position at the school had been confirmed. I had been the only applicant they interviewed on the day I went and I believe that the fact that I said I hoped to stay long term and make the village my home caused them to offer me the job on the spot.

I couldn't have been more pleased. The little house was perfect, with only two bedrooms but a neat living room and a large kitchen. If I had designed it myself I couldn't have done better.

The ceilings were quite low, but as I was only five foot four that didn't bother me. There was also no garden, but plenty of countryside around.

I thought I could be happy there, as long as I looked to the future and didn't dwell on the past.

Tamsin

We couldn't find her.

When we eventually asked at reception we discovered she had left while we had been looking for her. She must have come down in one lift as we were going up.

"Don't worry," I told Graham. "I'll write to her and explain everything. She won't like the phone. At least her reaction shows she still cares."

"I hadn't thought about it like that," he said, brightening up. "You're right. There may be some hope for me yet."

167

"Come on, let's join the fun. I want to tell you all about our new venture. Georgie and I are going into business together. You've got contacts in the holiday parks, haven't you? That one in Nottingham. They have entertainers?"

"I keep out of that side of things. They're more of a nuisance to people trying to take care of the forest. Mind you, I am taking up a position where we can accommodate visitors at the same time as caring for the environment. There's an area belonging to the City of London that I'm trying for. They're increasing their ranger team as it is changing from a Site of Scientific Interest to a Country Park – with a team of volunteers to help take care of the woodland. There's a lot of rhododendron clearing to do. In fact, there's years of work there, and it isn't too far from my parents."

"You aren't going to live back at home?"

"No. I've got a little terraced cottage. It needs doing up but I'll enjoy that."

"Well, give me the address. I don't want to lose touch. I haven't given up on getting you two together again."

The dance band had started up and soon the party was in full swing.

It wasn't my kind of music and my thoughts turned to my latest discovery.

We had a record coming out soon and then a tour. I would be at some venues but not all.

I needed to catch up with 'Pink and Blue.'

They were singing at a folk festival at Broadstairs.

Maybe I'd find some more acts there.

Margaret

Teaching a mixed age group was challenging but exciting. I had to make my introductions appealing to three year groups and then set the appropriate work so that it almost became individualised.

What was most interesting was that having better readers in with those learning to read helped the slower ones, when I had expected them to coast and rely on their elders. Indeed, their reading was better than those in classes I had taught before where all the children were the same age.

Behaviour was better, too and the children seemed more co-operative. It was a lovely atmosphere to work in, although we had to walk through the village to the recreation ground to do physical activities as we only had a tiny playground.

That was fun – taking a crocodile of children through the streets with a couple of mums to help. We often had parents standing round the field watching us as we exercised.

Our favourite game was rounders and we sometimes had people clapping and cheering us on.

The school also hosted summer and winter fairs and was open in the evenings for adult classes and meetings.

Living in half of the building I found myself involved with almost everything that happened in the village and when I bought a little dog, I called Millie, from the rescue centre to keep me company I found a whole new set of friends through taking her for walks.

Burnham Beeches were ideal dog walking woods – not too much undergrowth and lots of waymarked routes.

They were the kind of trees that let in light so it was often dry underfoot when other forests would be damp.

I began to enjoy my life and forget about the plans I once had to be a wife and mother.

Graham

I gave Tamsin my address at Stoke Poges.

"What a funny place name," she remarked.

"It's a lovely historic village. I think I'll be happy there."

"I wish you all the best," she chirruped.

She was making a success of her life, I thought, but there was still something missing in mine.

The house was lonely without anyone else to share the space. I needed a companion.

What kind of dog would suit a forest ranger?

Not a terrier – they'd be digging holes everywhere. Not a spaniel – they'd always be in the lake.

I fancied a chocolate labrador and began to search the adverts for a pedigree. I knew better than to find one at a puppy farm. I would make sure I went to a proper breeder and had a certificate.

It took three weeks to find what I was looking for and I took home a chubby puppy which I called 'Bounder.'

He did, too – he bounded everywhere.

Tamsin

The band were delighted to see me. Their record had done reasonably well and Georgie had arranged for them to be filmed, ready for a possible album.

Lily had filled out a little. She still looked delicate

but not so gaunt.

She and Jake were an item as I expected they would be.

We went over the programme for next year and Jake sang me a couple of his new songs.

I felt proud and pleased that I had started them on the road to success but they weren't particularly commercial.

Georgie had agreed with me that we needed to promote a solo artist and get our new discovery onto a TV talent contest.

Her husband had given us an office in one of his London buildings and we were gaining a reputation as agents who cared about their clients.

At last I had found something that wasn't boring and gave me the chance to travel round the country, seeing new places and meeting new people.

I loved it. I enjoyed living in hotels, having my meals cooked for me, not having a timetable and being free to take a day off whenever I liked.

Georgie took over all the dull, financial stuff. No longer modelling, she had blossomed as a business-woman and seemed quite content to only see Gregory at weekends.

She was still striking, with a beautiful deep voice that sounded both cultured and welcoming on the phone.

We didn't go to much together, but the partnership worked – and we were making a profit.

Music was changing, clothes were becoming more flamboyant. I loved the new styles, the new sounds, the new energy.

This must be the best decade ever for popular music, I thought.

It certainly was for me.

Margaret

It was the Easter holidays and Millie and I were having a day in the woods.

I loved watching the way she raced among the trees, sniffing, hunting, jumping over fallen logs.

She was an obedient dog – half collie, half something else – a loving but energetic companion.

I told myself she was the reason I hadn't booked a holiday away for the summer.

I couldn't think of anywhere I would rather be – especially on my own.

I had offered to look after the shop for a week while my parents went on a coach trip.

They had an assistant and a Saturday girl so it wouldn't be hard work. It would be a change and I could take Millie with me.

She disappeared for a few minutes when we reached the edge of the woods.

I called for her. I didn't want her to run into the stream

Then I heard a man's voice. "Down, Bounder, get down," and turned a corner in the path to see Millie and a brown labrador twisting, turning and running in circles.

"Don't worry," the man said to me over his shoulder. "He's been done – he's just frisky."

But Millie could look after herself and snapped at the other dog when he got too close.

The man bent down to catch his dog by the collar and put it on the lead.

I called Millie and, as I did so, realised there was something familiar about the stranger.

He was wearing a green jerkin with a motive on the back. It was a forest ranger – and someone I knew well. It was Graham Harris.

At that moment he turned to me with a look of recognition on his face.

"Meg," he cried. "This is fantastic. What are you doing here?"

"I live near here," I retorted, "but I didn't know you did."

"I've worked here for months. It's lovely to see you. I wanted to explain about last time."

"Tamsin did that, in a letter. She ruined the day for me. Seeing you was a shock – especially with her."

"I wasn't with her. I came because she said I'd see you."

"I know that now. I didn't then. You look good."

I couldn't help it. He did. His face had filled out and his shoulders looked wider. The bookish wimp I had first met had turned into quite a handsome hunk.

Millie sat looking at me and I stroked her and fastened her lead.

"Do you fancy a drink?" asked Graham. "We can sit outside the pub."

I was thirsty. I had no reason to refuse.

"Thanks," I said.

He smiled, then, and it lit up his face and made my heart flutter.

I had a desperate desire to find out if he was still single. Surely someone had snapped him up by now?

The dogs were happy with a dish of water and we

drank our beers in silence for a while.

We started talking together and there was an embarrassed "You first," before he asked the question that had been in my mind.

"Is it just you and the dog?"

"Yes," I answered, and couldn't help grinning at the coincidence.

"What about you? Have you got anyone special?"

He sighed and reached across the table to rest his hand over mine.

"You are the only special person in my life," he said. "Please try to forgive me. I want to go back to how we were before."

Before I called off the wedding, I thought, before he cheated on me with my friend, before he betrayed my trust and destroyed my dreams.

"It won't be the same," I said at last. "But I would like to see you again. You can tell me all about life as a forest ranger."

"Oh, good grief, I ought to get back," he said. "I'm on duty in half an hour."

He scrambled in his pocket for a notebook. "Here's my number, and my address. Where do you live?"

"In the next village, at the school," and I told him the telephone number. Then, daringly, I said, "Come over for supper one evening. You can tell me what made you choose Burnham Beeches."

"It was fate," he laughed. "I've never stopped thinking about you, you wonderful woman. I love you."

He didn't try to come round the table to touch me. He just grabbed the dog lead and walked away on his familiar lanky legs – but his shoulders were back, his head held high and I knew as I watched him go that I still wanted to be his wife.

I must have looked drunk to the people I met on the way home. I was so happy I couldn't take the smile off my face.

"Oh, Millie," I said when I got indoors. "You are going to like him – very, very much."